CHASING WREN'S TALE

J. A. FALES

What's the perfect cocktail for romance on Hesiod Mountain?

One stubborn, limber yoga instructor, with bad luck and a vibrator named Mongo, who has lost her appetite for love and men. One **HEAVY METAL** loving, incredibly buff bad boy Berserker Wolf seeking vengeance for Odin with a capital V. And a super manipulative goddess with intentions that are not as charitable as they seem.

Add liberal amounts of laughter, sexual tension, and satisfaction. Shake, pour and enjoy.

.

"Love is the answer, but while you're waiting for the answer, sex raises some pretty good questions."

-Woody Allen

CHAPTER ONE

There was a touch of magic on Hesiod Mountain, something that made each flower rare and vibrant and the sunsets exemplary. Humans felt it skimming and buzzing along the surface of their skin while Supernatural creatures witnessed it, more profoundly, in their bones.

Some believed that this magic put them closer to their gifts and the gods from which those gifts came. Those who did not believe—and those not so keen on deification due to bad experiences with pushy gods—considered it a load of *def*ecation aka horse hooey.

Gunnolf and his younger sibling, Loki, certainly felt the goddess Freya's presence as their vehicles hummed up the winding road to the mountain town of Elation. Of course, only one unquestioningly trusted it, and neither of them felt the slightest inkling of the goddess's husband, Odin, despite his more powerful connection to them.

If you're wondering why it was so powerful—which already makes you, my dear reader, quite clever—I'll tell you a secret: Gunnolf and Loki were the sexy sons of Gunnar The Not So Sexy Berserker. Few folks are aware these days, but Gunnar's progeny became the first of an elite group. These red-eyed werewolves didn't give a single damn (or half a growl) about the moon because the god of raiding and wars had fixed them.

After the minor trade—although it did permanently

disgust his wife—of one blue eye to gain ultimate knowledge, Odin wedged the power to control transformation smack-dab in the middle of their whirly, double-stranded thingamabobs. You know, the stuff scientists later called—oh, what was it, now? It's something that rhymes with Troubled Felix. Hold on. I'm lubing up the hinges to the dusty brain vault—oh, yes.

DNA.

Over the ages, humanity warped the legend of Berserker Wolves. No one blamed us. It was just what we did when things didn't make sense. So, eventually, the entire human world repainted this anomaly, in our cave wall frescos and our continually revised history books, as men sporting animal pelts in battle.

It was probably for the best. The lie prevented things from being awkward for the two brawny, bodacious brothers, who became the sole recipients of Odin's gift of immortality. They lived on while family, friends, and warriors hurtled toward their expiration dates like a clown falling off the stairs.

While the circumstances mentioned made them rare, their egos—the eldest one's in particular—were about to be tested. The immortal siblings were on the precipice of discovering something shocking thanks to a centuries-old quest once tasked to Gunnolf by Odin's super pushy command.

The immortal Viking warrior werewolves, with their sprawling bachelors' mansion and popular Fenric Fitness gym chain, were about to find out the truth. They were not the rarest beings on the mountain. There was a special, stubborn someone out there with a once upon a time that would turn out to be far more spectacular than theirs.

As a matter of fact, though currently unaware, they

were already arguing about her.

***

"This is a new era, bro, " Loki said, tossing another log into the fireplace. "Berserkers no longer exist. Your traditions are dead. The business of raiding and pillaging died centuries ago—and corporate, Wall Street, bullshit arguments do not count. Let me hook you up with Glenda— she will help you get a handle on this incessant need to play Alpha and control everything."

Gunnolf ignored the foul language that came to mind—and the underlying sting of his brother's insult— while silently considering the man basking in the warmth of the stone hearth. Aptly named after the first mischievous fool, Loki embraced fast-changing times and technology— website design, sound systems, rebellion, etc.—and abandoned every other lick of sense with frightening ease. Now, he had the balls to reduce an Alpha's need for dominance to psychological issues.

In light of Odin's generosity, Loki's adamant denial of their heritage and his constant arguments about the inequalities and violence inherent in the old systems, bordered on the obscene. Gunnolf had staunchly vowed, ages ago, to make his younger sibling see the glory of the good old days once again.

Someday, the jovial fool would look back on their Berserker traditions minus shame. That thought had made it well worth the exorbitant cost of importing remnants from the Old World—stones, wood, and metal—for use in remodeling their home.

Of course, all of it had been in vain, thus far.

Other than the occasional need to spar, battening down the hatches on violent urges, his little brother remained blind. No doubt, he would still be calling Gunnolf

3

savagely old-fashioned when the twilight of the gods came, and the great cycle of all life, death, and denial began anew.

"Even someone as thickheaded as you must see how barbaric the concept of a thrall was in the first place," Loki insisted. "Slaves are illegal, now—hunting someone down over a blood debt incurred by one is downright idiotic."

At six-foot-five-inches, well over two hundred and fifty pounds, Gunnolf was a mountain of muscle—to be precise, a mountain two inches taller and thirty pounds heavier than Loki. When he glowered and growled, flashing his fangs, it was not for kicks and giggles.

"Ooh, so scary," Loki responded, rolling his eyes before continuing. "Plus, that disorganized creature who called herself Freya's priestess was clearly a fraud. When she opened her purse, I spied candy bars inside—three of them, Gunn—enough to give a personal trainer a heart attack. That vision she shared was probably nothing more than a dream brought on by indigestion and questionable blood sugar."

"The eating habits of Freya's vessel are immaterial," Gunnolf argued, taking another sip from the glass of honey mead he'd poured earlier. "Gods make no errors. Talk to the contrary insults powers far higher than you, brother."

"But these are modern times," Loki countered.

"Dates on a calendar mean little to deities," Gunnolf said. "An ancestor of the water nymph that murdered Halvdan lives somewhere on this mountain, and I must kill him. The blood debt to Odin is long overdue. Period."

"What if it is not a him you find?" Loki demanded. "The candy addict did not specify a penis, Gunn. For all we know, you could be rushing off to massacre the fairer sex."

"Which would bring things full circle, considering a female murdered our brother in the first place," Gunnolf growled his response. The idea of killing something soft and sweet had always bothered him.

"He was a half-brother and nothing like us." Loki refused to back down. "You have conveniently forgotten Mother's indiscretion—how she begged and pleaded for Odin to make Halvdan a wolf, too, so that Gunnar would not kill him."

"I forget nothing, and Gunnar was our father. Show some respect and call the man by his title. You have conveniently forgotten Mother began her life with Father as a thrall." Gunnolf responded, fighting the urge to deliver a slap to the back of Loki's stubborn head. "She won her place at his side through love and obedience. There were no attempts on his life—unlike Honoraria and Halvdan."

"Obedience, possibly—I am not so sure about the love, " Loki insisted, "and Mother was not pregnant when Gunnar took her. Halvdan was a heartless, arrogant killing machine that tore a woman with a visible baby bump away from her peaceful life. The Viking laws were heartless— what kind of female would knowingly accept the conditions of death or slavery for her child?"

"Halvdan was not so different from us," Gunnolf grumbled, rubbing tiredly at the light worry lines—which were never going away—in his forehead. "Heartless or not, we were all meant to raid, plunder, and kill for the glory of Odin. So, even if you are otherwise right…"

"If?" Loki challenged him. "Gunn, you know that I am."

"Even if you are, it changes nothing." Gunnolf rose from a plush black sofa trimmed with intricate runic scrollwork. He paced the floor in his socks, the thought of killing a female making him more nauseous by the minute. "Rules are rules. A life for a life, Loki—there is no room left for discussion."

"No room, my pale ass—it was Freya's priestess, not Odin's that reached out to you! Stop clinging to the past. I washed my hands of blood long ago, and Odin chose to forgive me. Maybe he learned something about compassion from my behavior."

"That has always been the problem with you," Gunnolf responded. "When you open your mouth, nothing but jokes and blasphemy come out."

"Which are one and the same because they are also the truth," Loki said. "If the gods are so displeased, let them strike me down, now—see what happens when I challenge them? Nothing."

"Much to my regret," Gunnolf answered.

"Fine," Loki added, "how about this, then? The priestess did not say you must find them, Gunn. She told us you would find them. Stop trying to change me and get a dictionary—those words do not mean the same thing."

"Semantics," Gunnolf snorted, waving his glass in the air. "That is now your weapon of choice. Time has softened your edges too much. You will soon be wearing panties and skirts, not just hiding behind them."

"Wearing skirts and panties would indicate I have a different gender identity. As an employer, you should be aware that is a protected status, not an insult," Loki remarked, prodding the glowing logs with an iron poker. "There is a word that sums up the primitive need to hurl gender-biased comments at others, you know. You might have heard of it—it is called sexism."

"Sexism?" Gunnolf shook his head, breaking into deep laughter as he noted the aggravation on Loki's face. "Careful, brother. You might want to tug your dress down a bit further. I caught a glimpse of your vagina just now."

"Liar—you know if I had one I would never leave the

6

house," Loki answered, grinning at the insult. "You are the one who should be careful. Gods forbid you should reveal a sense of humor in the midst of all that brooding. Some woman might mistake you for a human being for once in your life."

"Never," Gunnolf responded, shrugging. "The hearts of the wise were not meant to be cheerful."

CHAPTER TWO

"Son of a *bitch."*

Wren pushed the thin sheet from her shoulders with the expletive. She sat up abruptly in the inflatable bed from the corner discount store and slapped it with the palm of her hand. It protested the rough treatment through a pinhole developing on the side.

Swinging her legs off the small mattress, she ruffled bangs her married friend, Daisy, had recently talked her into and scrunched her nose in frustration. With wide eyes and a slender build, she should have anticipated the fringe making her look more like the timid orphan once cowed by daily beatings than a respectable twenty-nine-year-old.

Not that a dicey haircut was the worst of her worries after leaving the damned earplugs and sound machine at home.

Unless she was okay with showing up to the park as Wren of the Living Dead tomorrow morning, she *had* to do something. Another sleepless night was unacceptable. Her yoga sessions had been donated to the Charity Fair several months ago, and a decent crowd signed up for attendance. A good impression with even some of them could mean new business—a bad one earned her nothing but more of the same bad luck.

The whole point of crashing in her studio had been not lying awake in a dinky trailer while her creepy neighbor's dog barked its brains out all night. Sadly, it wasn't meant to be. The pounding and howling of aggressive music through the wall Fenric Fitness shared with Wren's Namaste Nest had become the new bothersome pooch. The racket was rapidly depleting her patience and an already questionable sanity.

Wood laminate flooring chilled the bottoms of feet with toenails painted ballet slipper pink as she tip-tapped them against it. She grimaced and rubbed at the slightly bumpy texture of her kneecaps, currently pointed up at the ceiling through cartoon-patterned cotton pajama pants.

The bottoms were tight and thin from a few too many rounds in the dryer, but they were still her favorite articles of clothing. After everything else she sacrificed, there was no way she'd part with her PJs.

The thin slivers of artificial light, coming in through the front blinds, started to bother her as she gnawed on her bottom lip. The gym next door was supposed to shut down around eleven o'clock. It was a quarter to one in the ever-loving morning. Someone else might have been able to deal with the voices and music, and, yes, she'd have been better off being that person—but she wasn't.

"You'd have been better off as a *million* other people," Wren fumed, tugging on a string of fabric near Scooby's tail, "the Queen of England, a grocery bagger—anybody. You can bet your yoga-booty all of them are sleeping like babies tonight."

Had her ex-fiancé, Steven, been there, the man would have said what he always had. She couldn't let go of anything. Daisy had been right about the bastard when she said any attempt at a relationship with that mustache-wearing hemorrhoid would be an exercise in futility. The slimeball had bruised Wren's ribs and taken her life savings to run off with a dancer whose cheap *nom de stripper* came from a can of soda.

After that, there had been little choice but to sell the lake house she'd inherited from Florence for the capital to keep Wren's Namaste Nest up and running. Then, other businesses started migrating to newer strip malls, and she spent whatever profits she had managed to save just to follow. Fast-forward to sleepless nights and trouble gaining clients, and it summed up the slew of bad luck since her mother died ten years ago.

Even minus the house, Florence's love had been a rare gift. Just when Wren thought her young life was over, the cantankerous senior showed up to salvage it. She'd rescued her from that strange orphanage, where Wren had been watched and beaten, daily, like it was some sick experiment, becoming the only family Wren had ever known. Not a day went by where she didn't miss the woman's outlandish fairytales, filled with giant-slaying elves and scary wolves, and their spaghetti Western and science fiction marathons.

Life was hollow and lonely without her—still, attempting a relationship to fill the void had been the worst mistake of her life. The sex had been painful and obligatory, Steven had tried to control her, and, afterward, humiliated her by telling half the town she was a freezer temperature mackerel in bed. On the bright side, it no longer mattered. She had come to the brilliant conclusion that her first trial run with a man would be her *last* one.

As a bonus, Daisy's repeated insistence—that there was something wrong with Steven, not Wren's sex drive— had landed her a battery-operated boyfriend. Mongo was fabulous. He never hurt her and always did what she wanted.

With a solitary sex life and potential clients to

impress, the only thing left bothering Wren tonight was a lack of sleep due to party music. No, wait—the word music was a stretch. It was a grown man making ominous gurgling noises over a distorted guitar and bass. Presumably, those sounds were words. The only one she'd made out so far was the name of a place she recognized vaguely from mythology. *Asgaard.*

"Maybe you *did* fall asleep," she mused, sarcastically. "You fell asleep, died of an aneurysm, and this is some flavor of Viking Metal Hell catered by Satan, himself—a man everyone else knows as Gunnolf Fenric."

Yep. That would pretty much explain everything.

Wren jumped up to pace. She couldn't help it—the frantic rhythm of guitar riffs and incoherent babbling fueled her spiraling thoughts. That space next door was the largest one in the whole plaza. God knew how many people had packed in there, partying their butts off with a meathead whose life's ambition was, apparently, running the loudest gym on planet Earth.

No, on second thought, that wasn't true—she was fairly confident this stunt tonight had been arranged expressly for her.

When his lawyer had swung by, uninvited, to chat about selling her space, she shot him down cold. The stiff, expressionless man in the tailored suit had abruptly ended the meeting, explaining, "Ms. Cavanaugh. I believe I should warn you: no is not a word that Mr. Fenric enjoys hearing."

Oh yeah? Well, that was just too damned bad.

Wren was not about to let another browbeating jerk come along and ruin her dreams. No ma'am, the days of being bullied and lied to were behind her. The Viking might not expect a fight, but—by God *and* Katy, bar the door—he was getting one.

She marched into the bathroom and flicked on the light, giving the clear knob on the sink a vicious twist. Water in motion, whether a trickle or a stream, soothed and strengthened her more than words ever could—that, along with weird periodical dreams about the lake, added to the suspicion that she might be a tad crazy. Sometimes she felt things in her bones, too, like a weird sort of energy running through them. The closest thing she could compare the sensation to was a live electrical wire.

After a quick glance at her tired face in the mirror, a face with a slightly pointed chin and round, mismatched eyes—one green and one blue—she perked herself up with a splash of cold water. Baring her teeth just for the hell of it, she growled and snapped them shut around the pretend flesh of a muscular man-butt in desperate need of kicking.

She might be small, doggone it, but she was fierce, and so was her name.

At least, it was according to Florence, who had assured her the Duke, John Wayne, would have never tolerated the original word following *child's name* on her birth certificate. Ran wasn't just some name pulled from mythology—it was what a lily-livered coward had just about always done in the Westerns. She refused to allow one ugly word to set a precedent for the life of her little girl, so they turned it into Wren.

"Honey," Florence explained, "people think a wren is puny because it's not an eagle, peacock, or dove. They might ignore it, but that's okay. It just makes the wren even smarter and more determined. Do you know what it eventually does, after waiting patiently and letting all those other foolish birds think they can ignore it? One fine day, when it's ready to sing, it puffs up its chest and opens its beak, and it hits them with a melody that's as loud as a doggone bullhorn."

"And that's just what I'm going to do," Wren answered, wiping away a tear.

She gave a stubborn-chinned nod, fully committed to marching over there and clearing the cobwebs from the man's ears. Sliding a set of invisible six-shooters into an imaginary gun belt in honor of cowboys everywhere, she picked up the key to the studio.

Wrens don't cry in the face of adversity," she said, unlocking the front door. "We *scream*.".

CHAPTER THREE

Gunnolf was incredibly pleased with himself.

His spur of the moment after-hours party to announce their intention of adding a bar had been a stroke of genius for multiple reasons. Primarily, it annoyed the stubborn yoga nut next door, but it also proved the townspeople's interest in the latest trend—a holistic approach to fitness that said goodbye, severity of self-denial and hello, lifetime of pleasures enjoyed in moderation.

"The little birdie has yet to bang on the wall," Loki, currently pouring shots for the first in a line of ladies, shouted over the music. "Are you sure your plan is working, Gunn?"

Gunnolf, towering over the heads of several attendees, raised an eyebrow. It was the same commanding look that had once inspired terror in the hearts of the fearless.

Loki mirrored the gesture, clearly mocking him.

"Her vehicle is parked behind the building," Gunnolf boomed over Amon Amarth. The sheer volume at which the band's music played threatened to give his immortal brain a splitting headache, but it was necessary. "She is there and most certainly angry."

Gunnolf still couldn't quite believe Wren Cavanaugh had rejected his relatively generous offer for her studio. Not just rejected it—their lawyer had quoted the woman, whom he described as diminutive, with an astonished look.

"Sir," he said, apologetically, "Miss Cavanaugh asked me to inform you to take all your money, wrap it around you like a security blanket, and jump off the far side of the mountain. Also, she refuses to meet with you in person."

While a man his size had no need for a security blanket, and no desire to jump from things, he did learn something important from the exchange. The woman next door was going to require special handling.

Of course, he wasn't as heartless as he pretended. The offer was sudden, and, most likely, not what she had planned. But the woman had declared battle. He was a Viking accustomed to victory in battle so, by Odin's teeth, he would conquer her.

Until Wren's Namaste Nest gave way to Gunnolf's pub, she would not know a moment's peace in her studio.

A shifter, with an orange and white fox tattoo stretching from her shoulder to her elbow, caught Gunnolf's eye as Loki handed her a drink. His thoughts shifted, for a moment, to a conquest of a different kind.

Her hair was a vibrant crimson below its black roots, and the body beneath her tiny leather dress was well sculpted. Ample breasts balanced out all her muscles nicely, and the hint of thick nipple rings beneath the fabric hinted that she wasn't averse to others playing with them.

It was always the same at parties. He and Loki would easily take three or four women back to their estate. After the first was chosen, several others would tumble all over each other like dominoes to make it crystal clear team sports were agreeable. And a night of physical activity would, no doubt, cleanse his palate after dealing with the disagreeable little shrew he anticipated landing on his doorstep soon.

"Don't get me wrong, Wren's a nice person—I went

to school with her." A woman's voice carried over the crowd, from near one of the weight racks, worming its way into Gunnolf's ear. "So I'm not bad-mouthing her, I swear. I mean, look, I know she had it tough growing up with no one but that weird old lady to raise her. I'm just telling you what I heard. Steven had a good reason for leaving."

Gunnolf wasn't normally one for eavesdropping, especially not to idle gossip, but the woman had said the magic name. To the best of his knowledge, there was only one Wren on the mountain, and Intel was valuable when a man found himself at war.

"Of course, there's a reason Steven ran off with Fanta—he was an asshole."

"Well, yeah, but what was he supposed to do? Wren was bad in bed."

"Wren teaches yoga; do you have any idea how limber that makes her? "

"Yoga is so not sex. Besides, Fanta and I used to work at the same club. I've seen her strip, honey—she's limber as one of those cute little monkeys in the rain forest."

"Charles from the bank said Steven emptied out Wren's savings account—and he gave her a black eye."

"Yeah? Well, it was a joint bank account that he cleared out, so you might say he had a right to. It was stupid of her, giving him access, don't you think? "

"Oh my God—you are such a heartless bitch!"

Gunnolf frowned. He rubbed at the stubble on his broad chin for a moment and glanced in the direction of the two women who had been talking. Technically there was only one, now. The second stormed toward the makeshift bar, putting a good deal of space between her and the first. What kind of man hit a woman and stole money from her? He was just contemplating going over to ask her for more details when the adamant banging at the front door changed his mind.

"The game is afoot!" Loki shouted, picking up the remote control for the music as he grinned at his brother over the crowd.

Gunnolf merely nodded. His eyes locked on the entrance as the music subsided, his big body pushing through the throng of strangers. Nothing in the room compared to the lithe, lovely creature pounding at the axes-and-helmet logo etched in the front glass. He half-feared, if he looked away, the pissed off pixie, with her long dark hair and bare feet, would vanish.

Wren Cavanaugh's bangs and height might have made her appear an innocent thing. The breasts beneath her thin white tank top, with the light above the door shining down on them, did nothing of the sort. Those delicate mounds—ripe, firm, and gorgeous—redefined his idea of perfection.

Pert pink nipples the color of cotton candy teased him, daring him to imagine the feel of them between his lips and on his tongue. Something told him, once he tasted any part of this woman, he would never want to stop.

She was the creature he was supposed to believe worthless in bed, lacking in passion? It was impossible! He didn't care what rumors some malicious harpy had been spreading. Whoever this Steven person was, the fault was obviously his—and the man's loss was going to be Gunnolf's gain. Diminutive hardly did her justice. Why on earth had his lawyer not said breathtaking beauty, instead?

Mustering what he hoped was a warm expression, he unlocked the door and peered down into the most extraordinary eyes he'd ever seen. One was green and one blue, the colors of the ocean and sea. She smelled of jasmine and fresh, salty air with just a hint of spice. All thoughts of warfare fell to the wayside—he would offer her three times what the place was worth if she asked him to.

His priority was no longer talking sense into this remarkable woman now shaking her head at him. His body—and the Berserker Wolf inside of him—demanded that he pick her up and take her to his bed.

"You must be Wren," he said, leaning into the doorframe and sniffing intently at that glorious scent to satisfy his wolf. "It is a pleasure to..."

And that's when the little woman cut him off. Rising onto her toes, she poked a finger at his chest and bellowed like a drill sergeant taking on a recruit.

CHAPTER FOUR

Wren counted the cars and motorcycles in the parking lot with a shiver as the door to the studio clicked shut behind her. She banged the back of her head against the window with a tired groan. Gym magnate, bully, pied piper of idiots—would her list for Gunnolf Fenric ever stop growing?

"Great," she said. "This must be *some* stinking party."

There wasn't much she wouldn't give to have even a third of those drivers helping with the poor turnout at her classes, but facing them all in her ratty pajamas wasn't going to help. Especially not the owners of the cars she recognized.

The vehicles belonged to two, possibly three, judgmental biddies that had thrived on rumors and gossip about her for the past ten years. Adopted freak, closet lesbian, ice queen—anything their small, bored minds could think of had been fair game.

It was chilly outside, at any rate. Maybe she should go back inside and throw on a pair of jeans and a hoodie first?

No.

If she stepped back inside, she would most likely stay in there all night, a sleepless, cringing coward. If Florence had taught her anything, it was that fear was the worst of all four-letter words. Wren might be a fool, but she hadn't been raised to be a cowardly fool, and she wasn't about to start now.

With her head held high, she progressed past the closed blinds at the front of the gym, approaching the locked front door. The sounds of laughter and chatter inside seeped out, scraping over her nerve-endings the same way the music had while she was lying there, trying to sleep.

"You've got some nerve, Fenric," Wren muttered.

She peered at the bodies flirting and mingling through the glass and caught a brief glimpse of fiery hair. It belonged to the woman who came by to offer condolences after Florence's funeral—what was her name again? Sylvie? She said she and Florence had been friends a long time ago, which Wren found curious because the woman obviously wasn't old enough for the *long* part to be true.

Wren sighed, pushing the mystery of Sylvie's lie aside. She slammed the side of her closed fist against the door like a battering ram. The bones of her wrist absorbed the impact as she waited for Gunnolf to come. No more avoidance—time to confront the man head on and be done with it. Although she suddenly realized she'd never seen so much as a picture of the business owner before. There were plenty of buff men wandering around inside—which one was he?

A pair of rippling shoulders in a close-fitting t-shirt wandered through the crowd in answer to her question. Wren flinched. On second thought, dear God, he wasn't a man, and he wasn't wandering, at all. This barrel-chested *mountain*, with tree trunks for arms and legs, was stalking her with conviction and purpose.

Intense blue eyes, eerie and fascinating above high cheekbones and full lips, locked on Wren with the pull of a tractor beam. She felt their insistent tug all the way down to her toes. It was especially strong in her vagina, and, holy shit—that kind of reaction to a man was brand spanking new for her.

She shook her head to clear the distracting images that suddenly leaped to mind—his lips against her naked skin, those blue eyes hovering above her while she called out his name. Sexy sex with a big, sexy—*no, bad Wren, what is wrong with you, you pervert*—enemy. The treacherous thoughts lingered for a moment longer before, thankfully, her ire returned.

First, Wren got mad at herself—then him for making her think such dirty things. Who did this behemoth with his mane of thick hair and super-muscular physique imagine he was, subjecting her to his silent psychological warfare? The closer the man came, the more her resolve hardened—along with her devotion to her monogamous relationship with Mongo.

She ceased banging at the door, her heart threatening to thump its way out of her chest, as he turned the lock and opened the only barrier between them. He stood there, for several painful seconds, towering silently over her, with a snarling wolf tattoo on his right arm and a snarling helmeted warrior on his left.

So much foreboding, she thought, shaking her head. The beast probably had a gigantic, snarling penis in his pants, too. As if in answer, the corners of his lips lifted ever so slightly above the reddish-gold stubble dotting his jawline and dimpled chin. Okay, maybe it didn't snarl, but she was not allowing herself to think about his penis anymore.

The dimple was off limits, as well.

He leaned into the doorframe. His nostrils flared several times in succession as he inhaled deeply, angling his head in her direction.

What the—was he *sniffing* at her? Oh, God. He was

trying to tell her that she stank. That was so rude.

"You must be Wren," he rumbled, his voice decadent and deep as a second helping of chocolate cheesecake. "It is a pleasure to..."

"Listen up, you hulking varmint, and listen well." Freeing herself from the man's wicked spell, Wren stood on her tiptoes and used her bullhorn voice. A pink-painted finger poked as far up his shirt as it dared in conjunction. "Because I only aim to say this once."

An unexpected jolt of energy shot through her hand when she touched him. *Sweet Jesus.* The man was toasty-warm and solid as bedrock. She jerked the finger back, cradling it for a moment. Her eyes were the size of saucers, and she was pretty sure they were the *flying* kind, not the dainty ones people sometimes used for teacups. Her imagination took over again—this time, picturing every inch of him naked and that big chest pressed against her back as he tickled her neck with his lips and tongue.

She cleared her throat.

"Your music is crap," she powered on, hoping the man didn't understand why a rosy blush now flushed her cheeks, "and you can save your stupid, insulting intimidation tactics for somebody else. I, sir, am a liberated woman, and I will *not* be intimidated by the likes of you."

Gunnolf stared back down at her, sniffing again. He remained silent, but his eyes widened slightly and his grip on the doorframe increased, the knuckles turning white.

"Who do you think you are, some over-aged frat boy?" Wren settled back on her heels, getting into the swing of berating him, again, with her hands on her hips. The music stopped, and the room inside grew deathly still. "I have had just about enough of your loud, party-boy shenanigans tonight. Some of us are trying to sleep, for

God's sake."

The giant furrowed his brow, his eyebrows dipping in displeasure at the insult, as he pointed out, "I am not a boy, and this is not a residential area. It is a strip mall. You are not supposed to sleep in a strip mall—you go home for that kind of thing."

Wren looked up at the light above her, and the night sky beyond that, and asked herself what she had ever done to make the Universe treat her so horribly. She looked past the begrudgingly attractive wall of muscle into a room filled with exercise equipment, bared skin, shot glasses, *and* fans of god-awful music—only to find every last pair of eyes in the room staring right back at her.

I assume that you do have a home, Miss Cavanaugh?" he pressed, exploiting the advantage she had just handed over to him.

She didn't answer right away. She was too busy mulling over what sort of gossip would be circulating about her in the next few hours. Insane party-crasher? Yoga nut? Homeless weirdo reduced to sleeping in her studio? Or would it be all of the above?

Yeah, come to think of it, it probably *would* be all of the above. She'd have been better off holing up in her stupid trailer tonight. Sure, she would still be tired tomorrow, but the creepy neighbor's hyperactive terrier couldn't spread rumors that were bad for business.

Splendid.

Steven had taken her money. The Jordan family had bought her lake house, and she had just willingly handed over the last remaining shreds of her dignity to a gigantic Viking asshole.

The Universe definitely hated her. It hated her on the sole basis of her having the audacity to live and breathe within its hallowed boundaries. And, okay, in the interest of being completely honest, she had grown incredibly, depressingly, and overwhelmingly tired of fighting it.

But you are not a quitter, she told herself, *and you will get through this—as long as you don't shed any more tears. Whatever you do, don't cry in front of this gigantic, horribly inconsiderate—unbelievably sexy (no, stop thinking that)—man.*

Wren ducked her head and rubbed at the corners of her eyes, scrubbing the momentary wetness away as if it were an itch. She took a shuddering breath, squared her shoulders, and tilted her chin. Telling herself that the handsome bastard saw nothing but tiredness, she looked up at him and answered matter-of-factly.

"You're right," she agreed, "I *do* have a home, and I should go there. I've got a big day ahead of me."

Then, she turned on her heel and stumbled to the studio, sincerely hoping she could make it out the back door and home to her modest trailer intact. It would suck, ending up in the local paper as the exhausted business owner who died crashing her car into a ditch in the wee hours of the morning.

CHAPTER FIVE

Gunnolf stepped out onto the sidewalk, staring after the little yoga instructor as she entered a cheery storefront with nest eggs painted on its window. Interested in nesting, was she? He would be happy to let her do that in his king sized mattress. Mad as she was, his wolf recognized her arousal. An unexpected turn of events, but there was no mistaking it—she had wanted him just as badly as he did her.

The sign on her storefront said *Closed for the Weekend*, and it was technically Saturday morning now. What had she meant by a big day ahead? Probably nothing, the woman was beautiful but obviously insane. She had to be, smarting off to a man his size that way.

Still, Wren Cavanaugh wasn't just any run-of-the-mill lunatic. She was an undeniably sexy, demented pixie with the courageous mouth of a Valkyrie. A tasty-looking one, from the front *and* back, considering her tits and the way those pajama bottoms clung to that luscious ass of hers. He reached down to adjust his erection, trying not to think about how badly he wanted to howl and chase after the damned thing.

Her determination was admirable, especially considering the wetness in her eyes. Thinking back on it, he was surprised she chose to hide her tears. Many females in her position would have used them. Maybe she was too proud. Or did she think him completely insensitive?

Steven had been insensitive—it was doubtful she would agree to sex with another insensitive man.

"A good thing the little birdie had no weapon," Loki said.

Gunnolf turned from his disturbing thoughts to find his brother standing behind him, with his arms crossed and a shit-eating grin on his face. Not surprising. The only thing Loki seemed to enjoy more than giving him hell was watching those rare instances when someone else was brave enough to do it, instead.

"She is angry at you, too," Gunnolf growled. "This is a family business, remember?"

"I am not the one who sent a lawyer with the personality of a cardboard box next door to bully her. And I am not the one the little birdie was shrieking at." Loki's words came with a sharp, congratulatory slap to a massive deltoid. "Either way, she is gone, and I see no point in your standing outside. That is not where the pussy is, brother."

"Finally," Gunnolf said as he turned to head back inside, "a word or two of wisdom from that mouth of yours."

Gunnolf closed the door behind them, leaving it unlocked as the first in a series of signs that the party was ending. Someone had turned the music back on. He strode back through the throng, throwing open the heavy door to the office. Leaving it open behind him, he cranked down the secondary set of controls for the audio to half-volume. A twinge of guilt hit him—*fine*, another twinge of guilt—over the idea of the pajama-clad woman in tears.

He shook off the thought with a rare smile. Talk about psychological warfare—the little woman packed a lot of punch without even exerting much effort. She hadn't been trying to make him feel remorse, and, yet, here he was, wallowing in a wolf-load of it.

"Your brother says the party is wrapping up soon."

Gunnolf turned at the sound of a familiar voice—but familiar from where? The woman who had slipped into the office behind him had twin Pocahontas braids framing her face, and she complimented a pair of short shorts with an abbreviated tank top. The hem of it ended well above her flat, spray-tanned abdomen. Her braless, bouncy torso and the red lips offset by a much darker outline rounded out a look Loki fondly dubbed "stripper appeal."

"My brother is right," Gunnolf answered.

The woman shut the door behind her and sauntered over to him. She licked her lips, running a brazen palm over the bulge in his crotch. He looked down at her body, silently, suddenly realizing why he knew her voice. Pushing back a flash of anger—vile as she was, she did not deserve his violence—he considered, instead, what she was clearly offering. No doubt, Loki had sent her for tryouts because she had inquired about coming home with them.

"Well," the woman purred. She undid his zipper and tugged his jeans and Fenric branded boxers down around his powerful thighs, "It wouldn't be right to let you go without thanking you for your hospitality."

He watched red-tipped fingers wrap around the girth of his shaft. The woman swirled her tongue over the slit at the top and lapped up the salty moisture leaking from it with a lusty moan. Calculating eyes looked up, locking with his, as she took his dick into her mouth and sucked it, pure confidence curving the edges of her lips into a smile.

He raised his eyebrows at the temptress routine, and she furrowed her penciled-in brows in return. She had expected a warmer reception. With one hand still on his shaft, she broke eye contact and reached down to cup his balls firmly, stroking them and relaxing her throat to accommodate more of his shaft. Her eyes glanced back up hopefully.

His expression hadn't changed.

The woman hollowed her cheeks, now desperate for some sign of approval. The bobbing of her head over his dick increased. Hair fell out of her braids, her lipstick smearing everywhere, as she heightened the pace, determined to make him cum. The lips on his cock made loud smacking and slurping noise. His member tapped the back of her throat, several times, as she worked harder and harder, grunting and massaging his testicles with urgency.

Eventually, the familiar tingling at the base of his spine began. His balls tightened as the woman continue to work him, milking his cock with her mouth. He came without warning, shooting his load down the back of her throat.

Apparently, she was not the biggest fan of swallowing—she tried pulling back but didn't quite make it in time. Afterward, she tried to pretend it didn't matter, wiping her mouth and looking up with a forced smile. Her eyes were expectant.

Gunnolf stared back at the woman, considering her carpet-abraded knees, swollen lips, and the makeup smeared from here to Valhalla. She had gotten him off, but her touch was nothing special—the truth was, it was nothing, at all, in comparison to what he'd felt from one small finger on his chest. Along with a pass to the after-party, he wondered, what was this woman expecting to gain from him? Gratitude? Glowing praise? Infatuation?

There was no denying that the female *did* have quite the mouth on her. It was a large, vicious appendage capable of at least two things—sucking cocks like a champion and spreading vicious gossip and lies. She had already used those lips well, flapping them all over the place to slander Wren Cavanaugh before setting foot in his office tonight.

"I..." the woman frowned up at him, realizing he had no intention of helping her off the floor. "Aren't you going to say something?"

Gunnolf stared back at her, his blue eyes cold as she climbed to her feet. He glanced over the backstabber's shoulder at the open doorway. An impatient Loki stood there, with the fox shifter and two other wide-eyed females at his side. Gunnolf noticed, with a smirk, that his brother was the only one looking at anything above his waist.

"So?" Loki cut to the chase.

He flicked a slow, humiliating gaze over the woman who had so desperately serviced him. He pulled his pants up and zipped his fly, thinking of long dark hair and goofy pajamas.

"This creature is not worth the effort," he said, his voice flat, as he exited the room.

CHAPTER SIX

Wren shook her head as she glanced at light posts glaring at her from the plaza in her rearview mirror. Well, most of them glared. The one in the far corner just flickered on and off weakly—the same thing it had been doing for days now. Much like her life, the bulb was on its last leg and in desperate need of replacement.

Other people had begun to leave, but several cars still sat there, scattered around the parking lot. Which one belonged to the inconsiderate gym owner? It was the most expensive one, no doubt. Coming face to face with Gunnolf—and, oh, what a good-looking face it was—had been disturbing for all the wrong reasons. She was deeply disappointed in her body for reacting that way. Hell, up until meeting the arrogant bastard, she hadn't even believed her hormones had an overdrive setting.

"What gives the man the right to have that voice—and be so gorgeous?" she muttered flicking on her turn signal and watching her headlights chase shadows from the road.

His Scandinavian accent, with a rise in pitch and a slight roll of the R, had turned her name into a melody. Not that his unbelievable hotness, linguistic or otherwise, mattered. Wren reminded herself, renewing her focus on the road ahead, that man was a bully—an absolute monster, without a selfless bone in his body, on a mission to ruin her life.

She needed to talk to Daisy, now, more than ever. It was too late to call and unload on her, but the curvy mother of three had promised, earlier in the week, to come by the park post yoga sessions for a chat. A contact of Daisy's supposedly located details on a woman who had worked in the orphanage—a difficult task, considering the place burned down after Wren's adoption. They were all hoping this former employee had a clue about Wren's origins.

A second glance in the rearview told her that the crack she'd been ignoring in the lower right-hand corner of the back windshield was spreading. It had grown a network of little fingers, preparing to bloom into an angry web, soon.

She had toyed with the idea of replacing more than just the windshield. Did she dare? If she bought something, anything, the purchase would have to be a used model from a reputable dealer. Still, even five-years-old instead of twenty would be a godsend. A vehicle with a dent in one fender or a smattering of scratches would ensure that the kids from the back of the mobile home park wouldn't be interested in tagging or trashing it.

"Then again..." she muttered, drumming her fingers on the steering wheel as she thought about the pile of pastel yoga mats in the back seat next to her overnight bag.

A new windshield, let alone another car, took remote seating on her list of priorities at the moment. Building her business still sat squarely at the top, along with yoga mats. If any of the attendees forgot their own in the morning, she had them covered. Only it wasn't in the morning—it was in just a few hours, now.

Of course, it would be difficult to focus on standing up, let alone the practice of yoga, but she would not fail. All monies from both of the thirty-minute sessions were going to a women's shelter down in the valley. She had donated possessions, too. The knowledge that Florence's things—and many of her own—had helped families start over eased the sadness of donating them once the realtor accepted the offer for the lake house.

A hooded figure hanging out by the front entrance with an aerosol can in hand appeared in the glare from her headlights. It dove back into the shadows, and she kindly returned the favor, pretending not to have seen anything. Rest was what she needed, not a phone call to Dispatch to share idle conjecture over the intentions of a lone tagger in possession of spray paint.

Maybe it would be artwork, for once—at least, that was a sign of creativity.

"See no evil," Wren announced, shaking her head, as she parked her car in the driveway. "Too bad they can't paint the neighborhood quiet."

When she had first moved in, she spent countless hours fixing up the used trailer to make it feel like home. The effort made her circumstances bearable—it felt like she had a little peace, and some control in her life again. Then the creepy guy next door brought home a hyperactive yapper with an odd knack for digging up seashells and river stones where there shouldn't be any.

The little dog in question, now resting in its small yard by the chain link fence, opened one eye and sniffed the air in her direction.

"What?" she whispered. "Do you think I stink, too?"

The terrier pup—Daisy's husband claimed it was a Bichon Frise, but that was far too pretentious for a park mutt owned by a guy named Bud—closed the eye and placed a paw over its face. For once, it appeared to be as exhausted as she was. Whatever the reason, Wren was grateful.

She tiptoed around to the back door of the car and retrieved her blue overnight bag with the white straps before mincing up the steps in her bare feet and pajamas. She unlocked the door, crossing her fingers when the contents of her keychain jingled.

"Please," she muttered, sidestepping a sharp-edged coffee table in the living room, "just be a good little doggie for me, and keep your lips shut for a few more hours."

Certain she was too tired even to say the usual goodnight to Mongo, she stumbled in the direction of her bedroom in search of sleep.

CHAPTER SEVEN

"Oh, my Gawd!"

The raven-haired woman in the white bustier and abbreviated denim shorts squealed the words and plucked rhinestone-gilded stilettos from her feet. She dropped her shoes on a rack by the door, spun a barefoot circle, and trotted back to Gunnolf.

"A wrought iron gate," she said, "and now this? Your place is fantastic, Gunny!"

"Thank you," Gunnolf grunted, instantly hating his new nickname.

Despite having heard the woman being called by her name twice on the drive home, Gunnolf still had no idea what it was. Nor did he care. He did know a few other things about her. She chewed watermelon-scented gum incessantly, her toenails were an eye-gouging orange, and her voice was incredibly nasal.

"Amazing is an understatement," Sylvie, the redheaded fox shifter, remarked. She wrapped her arms around the waist of the third woman, a platinum blonde Loki had chosen. The blonde leaned back against her with a nod of agreement.

"You have armor and weapons on display," Sylvie continued, "and they look old. Am I right in assuming this is all authentic, Gunnolf?"

"Yes." Gunnolf nodded in the direction of the case

34

with an axe named Shield Breaker and his favorite sword, Thruster. The ancient Vikings had been a shamelessly literal people. "These things have been in our family for centuries and seen many battles."

"They look like they should be in a museum," the blonde said, pulling Sylvie's hands up to play with her breasts. "Aren't you worried someone will steal them?"

"Why in Odin's name would I do that?" Gunnolf frowned at the blonde, thinking she must be either joking or insane. "They are safer here than in some anemic curator's palms. This estate has a top-notch alarm system and, I assure you, anyone that dares steal from us will be dealt with most harshly."

Loki cleared his throat as soon as Odin's name came up. He grabbed a remote control and the room immediately came alive with the intro to Flight of the Valkyries, successfully circumventing any talk of gods or disembowelment. Then, he tilted the chin of the blonde, whose breasts were being expertly kneaded and massaged through a very thin top, giving her a wink and a slow, deep kiss.

"If you think what you see down here is something," Loki said, moving to the bar in the far corner of the living room, "just wait until we all head upstairs. The windows come with an even more spectacular view of the lake."

"Hey, is that classical music?" the dark-haired, fruity-breathed woman inquired.

"Yes," Gunnolf, who was growing more irritated with her by the second, responded before Loki could. "Wilhelm Richard Wagner—why?"

"Oh, no reason, I guess," the woman shrugged and plastered a smile on her face. "It just seemed like old people music, and I thought you two were hardcore Metal guys."

"This stuff is considered old now, pet," Loki interjected, jingling fresh ice in a cocktail glass to summon her as if she truly was one, "but it certainly wasn't back then. Hard as it may be to imagine, this music was the rock n' roll of its day."

The fox-shifter laughed out loud, a deep, throaty sound, and pushed the blonde girl in Loki and the raven-haired ditz's direction. She traipsed over to Gunnolf with a secretive smile and looked up at him. Her amber eyes twinkled as she swirled her index finger, in a repetitive circle, a hair's breadth away from his heart.

It was the exact spot where Wren had touched him not long ago.

"You must forgive our disbelief," she talked to the room but winked at him. "After all, I'm sure there are things in the world even you will find hard to imagine—and Wagner is ancient history for most of us."

Gunnolf stared back at the unmated shifter. He gave a silent shrug, indicating he had no idea what she was trying to say. Despite the redhead's peculiar behavior, he was certain of two things: She was the only female present who had no expectations of anything other than fucking, and he had grown tired of hiding his disgust with the gum-smacker. Fortunately, Loki was more than capable of entertaining two overly ambitious humans on his own— even if one was too fond of orange and probably prone to stalking.

"Come, Sylvie," Gunnolf ordered, allowing the wolf inside to turn his eyes red for a moment, "Up to my room. Now."

"As you wish," Sylvie answered, looking over at the bar. She was far less perturbed about the fact he'd immediately gone all Alpha than the other two women were. "But we need to have a little talk first, one that's going to require more alcohol. Have you got any up there?"

"No," he frowned. "This is a home, not a hotel—I do not maintain a bar in my room."

"Do you, at least, have two cups upstairs in this non-bar of yours?" she asked.

"Yes," Gunnolf said.

"Good," she beamed at him, "less for me to carry. Just let me grab us something reasonable to drink, and I'll be right behind you."

After grabbing the bottle Loki tossed to her, along with a not-so-subtle invitation to follow the sounds of all the panting and moaning to his room later, Sylvie followed Gunnolf up to the second story. He paused outside his door to point out, in case she was curious, that his room was at the far end of the floor from Loki's.

"Based on what I saw in your office," the shifter replied as he ushered her in, "I doubt that I'll be needing him."

She walked to a table inside, set the bottle down, and tipped an inch of aged Scotch into two glasses. Taking one in hand, she offered him the other.

Gunnolf took a sip from the glass and set it down. He wove his palm in the vibrant hair at the base of Sylvie's skull, tilting her neck back to make eye contact.

"You will not be the one in control here," he said. "You understand this?"

He watched the fox's gaze lower respectfully to his throat. Her mouth curved with the hint of a smile when he teased her pierced nipples with the lip of his cup through the material of her dress.

"Pack or not, you are an Alpha," she responded. "I would expect nothing less, and am happy to serve, should you still want me to, after our discussion. There is something of great importance that must be said—and, trust me, you'll want to hear it first."

"What?" he growled, curious as to what a horny shifter would deem more important than sex. "Speak."

"It's about the yoga instructor, the one whose studio you want to buy—Wren."

"I know her name," Gunnolf answered. He set his glass on the table and sank into one of his chairs. "Go on. You have my full attention."

"Good," the fox answered, settling across from him. She took a deep breath and a long sip of alcohol. "There was a time when I was very close to Wren's adoptive mother, Florence. Before she decided to care for the girl, she was something more than human, you see, and we shared each other's secrets."

"Such as?" he responded, folding thick arms over his chest.

"Such as Wren being a descendant of the water nymph, Honoraria. She is the one you've been looking for— the heir to your blood price."

He gaze settled on her face with the weight of a stone. She expected him to believe that the woman he wanted more badly than anything else in the world was the one person he must murder to avenge his family and appease Odin.

"You are lying," he said.

"No," she assured him, "I'm not—I will explain everything to you, but the story of Wren's life is more complicated than you might imagine. So I'm asking you, please. Listen to what I have to say, and think carefully before you come to a decision."

He sighed. If it were true, the gods had a twisted sense of humor. He would never hear the end of it from

Loki.

"Fine," he grunted, "get on with the tale."

CHAPTER EIGHT

"Oh, come on, already—this is ridiculous."

The dog in the yard next door hadn't made a peep. The silver colored sound machine on Wren's nightstand ebbed and flowed with the soothing sounds of water. Conditions were perfect, optimal for sleeping, so why couldn't she do it?

It made no sense after her drowsiness on the road.

Of course, after asking the question, she immediately knew the answer. Her traitorous body hummed with sexual frustration because her mind wouldn't stop revisiting the source—a sinfully sexy man, with red-hued stubble and piercing blue eyes: Gunnolf Freaking Fenric. His chest had felt like heaven, and she was dying to find out about the rest of him.

No.

This was not who she was. She was a proud, independent woman who had no use for a one-night stand or a relationship with anything other than cylindrical plastic. Besides, he was the same arrogant jerk trying to bully her into selling her business. Everything about him was W-R-O-N-G. His taste in music was deplorable, he had no concern for others, and he had sniffed her like two-week old garbage.

Steven had been an arrogant jerk, too, but...damn. Gunnolf's version was so much hotter. Those lips were plush and kissable, even when he used them to scowl.

Oh God, not the mouth—don't think about the man's mouth.

She pictured him wearing a plastic Viking helmet and brandishing a toy sword—an IQ starved idiot preparing to invade her like a replica of an English port. It backfired on her, though, when she went a bit too far and envisioned the invasion. At that point, fully aware there was nothing on earth that could put the brakes on her libido, she gave in, wrestling her pajama bottoms and panties down her eager hips and thighs.

Rolling onto her side beneath a sheet that smelled of ocean fresh fabric softener, she dropped both articles of clothing onto the floor. An inadvertent glance at the plainly framed picture of herself and a gray-haired, smiling Florence on the bedside table made her pause hopefully along the way—nope, still horny.

She turned it facedown with a gentle hand and sighed, sliding her body back against the mattress. Naked except for the tank top, Wren let the cool air fan her legs and the soft, hairless warmth of the mound between them. She never had to wax or shave it, though she had been told most women did. Not that he-who-shall-not-be-named-while-masturbating had ever bothered spending enough time down there for it to make a lick of difference.

She bit her bottom lip, angling her hips and widening the gap between her thighs. A lazy hand trailed down over the slope of her abdomen, the light touch of her own splayed fingers drawing goose bumps from the skin. Her long lashes fluttered shut, tickling her cheeks as she slid the opposite hand up beneath her cotton top, rolling the stiff peak of a nipple between her thumb and forefinger.

She pictured Gunnolf's face hovering above her and imagined his thick fingers touching her body. She was a plaything, now, his plaything, and, evil man that he was, he wanted to hear her beg. She gasped and arched her back, surprised at the strength of her own reaction as she pinched and tugged at a tender nipple, distending the hardened peak.

The hand on top of her mound crept lower, exploring the softness of her pussy. Its fingers stroked and teased more honey from between her nether lips. She dipped a finger inside, adding a second one before roughly plunging them inward. Her hips hitched in the air, a soft moan breaking from her lips to welcome the invasion.

Reaching up with her thumb, she worked her clit in a circular motion, gradually increasing the pressure. The feeling of her own fingers, their width inside of her, still wasn't enough—she needed to be stretched and filled. Pausing, she slid the hand free from under her tank top, propping her body up the side of the mattress.

"No offense, old friend," she breathed, ignoring the downward facing photo as she grabbed the only decent partner she'd ever known out of the drawer in her nightstand. "But I'm changing your name to Gunnolf until I get the asshole's weird sex-magic out of my system."

She lay back, sheathing the thick rubber dildo inside her slick walls, pumping it, in and out, with a happy groan. The motion was agonizingly slow and far too gentle for what she needed at the moment. Still, she took her time because she imagined he would.

"Gunnolf," she panted. "Please."

Saying the words aloud—the wicked feel of them on her tongue, the thought of him being there, using her and driving her insane—made her even wetter. Her opposite hand slid down, the fingers dipping into her dampness above Mongo before traveling back to her clit. She massaged it in time with the rhythm now building, now pounding, between her legs.

Wren strained and shuddered, her muscles growing taut. She focused on the arrogant face of her fantasy lover. The muscles in his shoulders and chest rippled and strained, his chiseled lower body thrusting as he fucked her. It was his voice telling her what a dirty little girl she was, telling her that she couldn't cum—she wouldn't cum—until he said she could.

When she finally did find mind-shattering release, it was his name she cried out before rolling onto her side.

Bereft of energy, she set the alarm clock with trembling hands and allowed the darkness to come, carrying her off for a few short hours of sleep. The last thought she had before unconsciousness claimed her was that an orgasm courtesy of Gunnolf Fenric had been just what she needed.

CHAPTER NINE

"So, you see," Sylvie said, "Florence was an elf, álfr in your native tongue, until Freya explained how Odin cursed every female of the nymph's bloodline. Every last one would suffer until the blood debt was paid. The goddess asked her to save Wren, told her where to find her in that horrible orphanage, so she did. Florence gave up everything and never regretted it—she gave that girl a mother's love."

Gunnolf stopped pacing long enough to peer out at the bright moon hanging above the lake. It was beautiful, but not nearly as much as the selflessness Florence had shown giving up her immortality for a stranger. Sylvie still spoke so fondly of Wren's adoptive mother, almost as if there had been more than friendship between them.

"I will not deny she was a remarkable woman," he nodded, clenching his jaw. "One I now wish I had known. But this does not negate the fact that Freya has spoken—I fear the time for kindness is gone."

He watched the reflection of the shifter, in the glass. She approached him from behind, pressing the taut globes of her breasts against his back as she leaned in to wrap her arms around him. Deft fingers undid the clasp and zipper of his jeans. Her body dropped in a fluid motion, sliding the denim down his thighs.

"Are you sure?" she countered as Gunnolf lifted his

feet, one at a time, to aid her in removing them. "The goddess may have spoken, but she is cunning. Her interests are not always perfectly aligned with Odin's. At its core, the concept of a blood debt is nothing more than the repayment of one life with another—yes?

"It is," Gunnolf confirmed, his voice muffled through the shirt he pulled over his head. "What do you have in mind?"

"Halvdan took Honoraria as his slave, right?" Sylvie asked, keeping up the line of questioning as she undid the clasp at the back of her neck. The front of the dress fell to her waist.

Gunnolf dropped his shirt to the floor and turned, still in his boxers, to slide a hand back into the fiery hair at the nape of her neck.

"Yes," he responded, pulling her head further back than he had before, until her breasts were thrust forward enough for his appraisal. "He took her—she murdered him and fled, displeasing Odin."

"Do you believe he cared for her?" Her voice held a tremor of anticipation. "Could it have been love at first sight?"

"I have no doubt Halvdan desired the nymph, but he was not like Loki and me. Father treated him differently, growing up," Gunnolf answered, releasing her hair to test the weight of her breasts. He squeezed them, hard, observing the way her breathing changed before flicking and tugging at the metal nipple rings with the little black beads in their centers.

"Our half-brother was notorious for his cruelty with bed slaves," he continued as she coaxed the rest of the dress from her lower half onto the floor. "His heart might have been distant, but, when he saw Honoraria, he wanted her more than he had others. It is not for me to say whether or not he would have been capable of seeing her as anything more than an amusement in time."

"Would you have treated the nymph as he did?" The Fox shivered as she spoke. Her voice grew ragged, her pupils dilating as his hand spanned her hip and delved lower. "Would you have beaten her, had she been yours?"

Gunnel paused in his exploration, staring back at her thoughtfully.

"No," he responded, sliding a hand into her panties and cupping the warmth of her pussy. It was already on fire for him, slick and willing, and her whole body trembled with need. "Thrall or not, I would never hurt any female as he did—a woman's body was made for pleasure, not abuse."

"So, the goddess knows you differ from Halvdan," she moaned, rocking her hips back and forth to ride the cradle of his palm, "yet, by Odin's will, there is a debt requiring payment."

He briefly allowed the blatant attempts to brush her clit against him. The room grew quiet except for her panting—lovely, wanton sounds—as she strained and rocked, desperate to find her pleasure. He slapped the curve of her bottom when he sensed she was nearing release.

"There are rules in this room," he reprimanded. "You will observe them. No cumming without my permission."

"Yes, Alpha." Sylvie acknowledged his wishes and stilled her movements, going back to their prior discussion. "So, it is clear that the obligation—a life for a life—must be met."

"That is not news to me," He responded wryly, tracing a vein that pounded in her neck.

"Then, this should not be either," she answered. "Odin deals in battle and death, but what is his wife's domain? Love. I believe Wren is meant to be yours—Lady Freya intends for you to claim her and love her, not kill her. Think about it: If the two of you created a new life, together, wouldn't it replace the one that was taken?"

Gunnolf raised an eyebrow, the plane of his face breaking into a bright smile. Sylvie's priority had not been sex, after all—no matter how badly she needed it. She had sought him out to explain how to save Wren.

It was a grand idea.

Aside from his brother, Gunnolf had survived without companionship, and he'd come to accept that was just the way things were. Never had he imagined a beast such as himself—the relic of a violent age, as Loki often called him—being worthy of anything more. A mate, a child, the prospect of domestic bliss, all of it had been out reach, out of the question. Yet, here he was, with a mate to claim, and that was just what he intended to do—mark her with the wolf's bite and give her a baby...women loved babies.

"So the rumors about foxes are true," he mused. "Sly and cunning as the goddess, herself. I cannot fuck you, now—not knowing that I have a mate—but I can still reward for your efforts. Remove your panties, and lie on the edge of the bed."

"I thought I could handle this," she answered, moving on shaky legs to pick up her things, "but I can't. Wren is Florence's daughter, and you are hers, now, every bit as much as she is yours. Don't worry about me—I'm going to head down the hall and accept Loki's invitation. My car is over at the city park, though. You can drive me there, later, if you don't mind.

Gunnolf nodded, relieved at her choice as she carried her things to the door. The least he could do was give her a ride.

"You know," Sylvie paused in the hallway to caution him. "You might want to tread lightly with the girl—and find space for your bar somewhere else. Florence was tenacious. She had to be—she was in the business of slaying giants back in the day. I'm sure Wren was raised to be the same. One male has already failed her miserably—beaten her, used her, and stolen from her—he made her the laughingstock of Elation."

"I am a warrior," Gunnolf answered, with a shrug of his shoulders, as he pulled back the sheet and climbed into bed in his boxers. "Easy or not, I will show her that she cannot defy the will of the gods."

"Good luck with that," Sylvie said.

"Close the door for me," he yawned. "I will see you in the morning."

CHAPTER TEN

Wren groaned as the eardrum-busting bleep bleeping of the alarm pulled her from the land of dreams for the second time. She rolled over and pried one eyelid open, preparing to slap the snooze button like it owed her money—another ten minutes and she would be spiffy. Then, something awful occurred to her. It wasn't the second time—it was the fourth.

"Shit!"

Goodbye, hopes of starting the day off by being in control of it. She sat up and rubbed the crusty bits from the corners of her eyes. The agitated yapping started on the outside of the trailer as soon as she slid out of bed. For once, she wished it had started earlier. Oh, well—time to make a mad dash for the shower, don cheery workout gear, let her hair dry on the way, and fake the rest.

In the shower, surrounded by the scent of sweet apple cider shampoo—the same stuff Florence used on her hair as a child—the barest fragment of a story wandered into her head. She was confident it was something from when she was still fairly young—waist-high to a grasshopper as Florence would have said. The tale started with once upon a time—which was no help at all because most stories started that way. What was the rest of it?

Once upon a time there was a lovely maiden, far away from the home that she loved...

Wren turned off the water and grabbed a towel, stepping from plastic shower stall that she'd scrubbed clean two sleepless nights ago. She had a morning's worth of activities stretched out ahead of her. There was no time to sprint down memory lane, let alone take a leisurely stroll in search of forgotten fairytales.

She buffed her body hurriedly with the thick cotton and, then, wrapped it around her hair. Twisting the towel into a long turban, she squeezed hard enough to sop up a bit of the moisture from her tresses before letting it fall to the floor.

Several minutes later, after Wren had stubbed her toe twice in the hallway and was suitably dressed, she dashed for the front door. The white yapper ran to the fence, snapping and snarling as she bounded down the front steps past it and into her vehicle.

Coffee would have been nice, but she forgot to set the machine the night before. There was no time left for grabbing any, not even at a drive-through window. Her nerves would have to carry her through her classes. After that, maybe she'd luck into a quiet space to nap until Daisy found her.

Her cell phone rang as she pulled onto the main road, and she answered with a hello.

"Hi, Wren. It's me."

"Hey, Daisy—what's up?"

"Something came up with the kids," Daisy said.

"Let me guess," Wren sighed, "you're not going to be able to make it today."

"Yeah, sorry, Wren—I can meet you for brunch next week, though. How about the Tea House, say noonish on Friday?"

"Alright," she said, "but you've got to promise me

you will be there. I really need to talk to you about the guy next door."

"The one with the dog?" Daisy asked.

"No," she responded, "not that jerk—a new one, the guy that owns the gym next door to the studio—Gunnolf Fenric."

"Gunnolf?" Daisy questioned the name. "Not a lot of those around—is he Swedish or something?"

"He's something, alright," she responded. "He's a pain in the butt, Daze, and he's trying to make my life completely miserable. I'll tell you the whole story when I see you."

As luck would have it (for once), Wren arrived at the busy park with about five minutes to spare. The events coordinators—a tastefully dressed, slightly judgmental woman—had saved her a parking space near an oak tree. It was close to the sound system and the grass where her sessions were. Wren slapped a ponytail holder in her hair, grabbed a handful of mats and bounded over to the group of women and one thin man waiting for her on the grass.

"Welcome and thank you for coming," she beamed at them as she kicked off her sandals and left out the bit about almost being late. "I'm grateful you've all shown up today to support the shelter. My name is Wren—as some of you may already know, I own Wren's Namaste Nest, over on Bear Claw Blvd."

"Isn't that next to the new gym, Fenric Fitness?" one of the women at the back of the group asked loudly.

"Yes, it is." Wren forced a smile in response to the name. Of course, someone would bring up that man at one of her sessions. "For those of you who'd like to learn a bit more about my studio, I'll be passing out flyers when we're through. Let's get started with some wonderful, healing sounds and a few sun salutations shall we?"

The first class went smoothly, as did the second, for the most part. Although the exhaustion she'd been battling started to kick in towards the end, Wren's body had been at the practice so long that the yoga itself was much like breathing. She just had to make sure her mouth kept moving as she progressed to the next pose, and then the next one, all the way to the end of the session.

A couple of cars came by the area as the class continued. The noise of doors slamming, engines purring, and conversations soaring over the music threatened to break her concentration. She didn't let it. Wren just smiled for all she was worth and spoke a smidge louder, hoping her bright turquoise yoga capris and sports bra were distracting enough that, even if something weird was going on with her face, no one noticed it.

After the class, a few folks asked for flyers—and two women, annoyingly, only wanted to talk about the sexy men that owned the gym next door. Had Wren met either of the owners yet, and weren't they just hot as hell? Wren smiled flatly and made a comment about the Hell part sounding about right before shooing them away so she could gather her things and take them back to the car.

The wave of severe exhaustion she kept pushing away finally hit her at full force as she lay her mat down beneath the sprawling limbs of an ancient oak tree. Now that the noise at her end of the park had died down, it was time to catch some Zs.

As she drifted off, a little bit more of the story came back to her: Once upon a time there was a lovely maiden, far away from the home that she loved. She was lost, and tired, and wandering aimlessly atop a great mountain...

CHAPTER ELEVEN

"Huh," the redhead told Gunnolf, "I could have sworn that I parked the car over here."

"That is the same thing you said twenty minutes ago, Sylvie," he growled at her smiling face in disbelief.

He was fed up with driving around in circles and fed up with pretending to be patient about it. A few more minutes, that was all he could tolerate before kicking her out of his SUV. Still, as frustrated as he was, something about her grin made him look in the same direction. Once he did, he saw the explanation for her behavior.

Wren.

"On second thought," Sylvie said, "never mind. I left my car here because of a few old friends I wanted to say hi to, anyway. You can drop me off right here—I'll find my way home eventually."

"Okay." Gunnolf responded succinctly, pulling his vehicle into a parking space—they'd had enough communication for one day, already.

So, this was what the little instructor had meant by a big day ahead. He turned off the engine, his eyes latching onto the cheery turquoise bottom she suddenly thrust into the air.

Round, firm buttocks pushed against a center seam in the back panel of the woman's yoga pants for several breathtaking moments. Her hips dipped down to the mat with a sinuous grace, the muscles of her back poised and arching beneath the sport bra. A light sheen of sweat glistened on her limbs and those ripe breasts jutted forward like an offering before she popped up and rolled through the motions all over again.

By the gods, Wren Cavanaugh was Valhalla in the flesh—that body was a banquet. Blood debt or not, he wanted to feast on her in every way possible and keep her for his own. This time, when she went into Downward Dog position, he pictured her naked in the pose, her legs spread wide and her pussy lips stretching to accommodate his upward cock.

Gunnolf shifted in his leather seat, adjusting to accommodate the sudden hardness pressing uncomfortably against the seam of his jeans

"Word to the wise: You might want to close your mouth before the wind kicks up, or it'll be gathering dirt and flies," Sylvie said, drawing to his attention that she was still there. She drove the point home with a humorous glance at his crotch before slipping out onto the pavement, in her leather dress, and closing the passenger door.

Gunnolf clamped his jaw, giving her a look that told her it was dangerous to talk to an Alpha that way. What she had said about visiting friends was probably a lie. She was going to call someone to pick her up and take her back to the gym, which was undoubtedly where her vehicle had been all along.

Sophie winked back at him, mouthing the words talk to her before pulling a cell phone out of her purse and strolling off to investigate the far side of the park.

"This would be far easier with a longship and weapons," Gunnolf grumbled drumming his big fingers on the steering wheel.

He lowered the windows, flaring his nostrils to catch the heady scent of Wren in the spring air as her body rolled through another sequence. Sunlight bounced off her soft hair, forming a halo around it. He blamed Freya for the sudden need to run his fingers through those silken strands, and for making his mate the most beautiful woman he had ever seen.

"Your sense of humor," he said, "has grown twisted, My Lady Freya. You would give me a prize destined to hate me as Honoraria hated Halvdan and make me want her badly as my next breath."

Listen with your heart, the goddess responded, not your fears—fear exaggerates the enemy.

Gunnolf didn't have long to consider the whisper in his thoughts before his cell phone buzzed in the center console, alerting him to a new text message. The thing was a sleek, lightweight model—according to the woman from the cellular device store, the latest craze. His brother had agreed, insisting on the ridiculous upgrade as soon as he discovered they must switch providers for decent coverage on the mountain.

Loki intended to take the two women from last night out to lunch down in the valley in return for helping him check out two gyms in the area. He anticipated not being home until late in the evening or possibly the next morning, which worked out well for Gunnolf.

He needed to take his mate somewhere private to talk with her.

With no loose women lingering at the house to give the wrong impression, the decision was easy. He would take her home and begin to woo her. The only problem now would be getting the little spitfire to come at all, let alone quietly. Then again, he thought watching her undo her hair, stretch out on a mat beneath a nearby tree, and close her eyes, it might not be too hard.

"Thank you," he told Freya quietly, smiling.

Gunnolf crossed his forearms and plopped back against the thick upholstery of the driver's seat. The goddess was finally placing him back in familiar territory. It would be the gentlest bit of pillaging he had ever done, but it was pillaging, nonetheless. He noticed the driver side window on her car was open—once she slept soundly enough, he would be able to grab her things.

He worked out the rest of his plan, knowing her driver's license would give him her permanent address. He would convince Loki to return her car and gather her clothes for an extended stay with them. On Monday, one of them would place a sign on her studio door declaring classes cancelled indefinitely.

"*Sof þú vel*—Sleep well," he said, "and rest, my tired little nymph. You need it. Your wolf will be claiming you soon."

CHAPTER TWELVE

Once all the attendees and stragglers had left, Wren set her mat down beneath the relaxing shade of a wide-armed oak tree. She wished Florence were still around or Daisy had shown up, today. They both would have been so proud of her. All their lectures about gumption and stick-to-itiveness—the ones telling her you're stronger than you think you are, so start acting like it—had paid off.

She'd done it, with not even one slurp of coffee and barely three hours of sleep under her belt to boot. Whether the struggle won her any new business or not, Wren had lived up to her end of the charity bargain. As far as she was concerned, it was time to tally her Saturday morning under the successes column.

Also, fair or not, the blame for her near failure resided on the hulking shoulders of one pain-in-the-butt, sexy Viking jerk. Wren intended to stay as far away from party boy Gunnolf Fenric as she possibly could from now on. If she had to deal with someone, the beast could send over his creepy, expressionless lawyer—the one who did absolutely nothing to her heart rate and hormones.

"Woo-hoo for me," she yawned, pumping a sluggish fist in the air. "This calls for a victory nap."

There was no need to get her cell phone and set the alarm. The events in the park had a decent turnout today— some stranger was bound to spy her lying out like buzzard bait and come along and disturb her momentarily. As annoying as that would be, the opportunity for some shut-eye still seemed too perfect to pass up. She could almost guarantee the pesky white pooch outside her trailer would be in rare form and raising all kinds of hell by the time she reached home.

Wren freed her hair from its twisted nylon band with a sigh of contentment and flopped her loosened spaghetti limbs on top of a colorful rectangle. The rich scents of the earth and wildflowers mixed with the familiar rubbery aroma of the practice mat, an unusual combination but one she found oddly soothing. Focusing on the act of breathing in, and enjoying the soft breeze on her skin, she slipped away into the land of dreams.

At first, there was darkness. Then, a burst of brilliant light came from the nothingness. Wren jerked up—technically, she swam up because the brightly colored mat she had fallen asleep on was now a body of water—and rubbed her eyes. It was the strangest thing. She suddenly found herself floating at the edge of a great river, watching a broad-bottomed ship—an impossibly long and large one, with a great mast and a dark red-eyed wolf on its flag—coming into view.

Large men with armor and shields poured off the craft into rowboats, and their eyes shifted to an eerie red as they rowed. Soon, they were howling in fury and taking the shore en masse. Berserker Wolves a voice whispered the word in the back of her head.

Whatever they were, these evil beasts were intent on raiding the village, taking innocent human lives, and burning everything that remained to the ground. Though her belly was great with child, and she had hidden here, out of the way, for safety, she felt an obligation to protect them.

The life inside of her was precious, but wasn't all life sacred? It made no difference to her that these creatures were not her kind. She needed to help them.

Wait—since when were humans not her kind?

Wren frowned, looking down at her reflection in the water. The face staring back at her bore some resemblance to her expectations, but it was still extraordinarily odd. The blue of the creature's eyes matched one of Wren's, but the sockets were wider and slanted too high. Her undulating hair was the exact shade as the dark reeds that swayed beneath the water. Her breasts were swollen, a sign of the life growing inside of her. Wren's lips moved as she felt her tail shift into legs—the legs grew chains and shed them, bloodstains appearing on her hands.

"Honoraria," she whispered.

Another face appeared in the water behind her—a dark-haired beast with a jagged scar that traversed the left side of his face. His eyes glowed red, and the blood of others covered him. He growled, turning into a wolf-man that lunged for her. As the monster leaped, her heart sank, gripped tight by an overwhelming sadness.

Somehow, she knew: Honoraria's brave efforts would not save a single villager from slavery or death that day. And, though her child and bloodline would survive, the innocent life the water spirit had once known would be gone forever.

The beginning lines of the forgotten tale echoed in the air around Wren as the water rippled below her. Once upon a time there was a lovely maiden, far away from the home that she loved. She was lost, and tired, and wandering aimlessly atop a great mountain. She watched as Honoraria's reflection shimmered and disappeared. A beautiful, golden-haired lady wearing a crown and a cloak of feathers replaced it.

At the sight of the lady's face, something else became clear.

The voice Wren now recalled, the one that had begun the most elusive fairytale of all—the story of an orphan's life—had belonged to this woman, not Florence.

Though the woman's eyes were kind, Wren blanched at the sight of another wolf creature, gigantic and fearsome, behind her. The thing that attacked Honoraria had been black—this one was even larger but white, with unblinking red eyes staring back at her. Wren's heart pounded, threatening to leap up into her throat and choke the life from her. She pictured that animal on a flag flying high above the water. The white creature was dangerous, and it was coming for her this time. Viking. Berserker. Wolf.

"My enemy," Wren murmured in her sleep.

The woman's reflection shook its head a bit sadly. It reached down to touch Wren's shoulder from behind. The smile on its face held Wren captive, soothing her fears and filling her with warmth and light.

"Sleep deeply, little nymph," its voice commanded. "Sleep deeply, and well, and when you awaken, we shall begin to right old wrongs and work on finishing your story."

The darkness reclaimed her, wrapping Wren up, again, in the velvety cloak of rest. She was secured by it and lifted—swept up high in invisible arms as she gently floated off into the breeze.

CHAPTER THIRTEEN

Gunnolf took his eyes off the road for a moment, glancing over at the figure snoring like a congested baby dwarf beneath the three-point harness in his passenger seat. The sound was cute and not overly loud. He had spent centuries listening to worse, at least, in the belly of boats and near campfires.

A happy smile curled its way above the reddish-gold stubble that desperately wanted to become a warrior's beard again. He and his wolf were in perfect agreement. Ours. Nothing could bother them, now. There was a connection between him and this little female, a magical tether between two hearts that would only strengthen over time.

Taking her had been a piece of cake. No, a glass of mead—Vikings didn't have cake, and badass buff guys shunned it. Regardless of the metaphor, nobody noticed and stopped him with questions. Wren hadn't awakened to yell at him, either. As a matter of fact, she had barely stirred when he lifted her, her face turning instinctively into the cradle of his shoulder, instead.

Of course, the goddess could not keep his dainty, snuffling mate asleep indefinitely. The battle of wills that the clever fox had predicted between them, one he had no doubt was coming, lay ahead. She was a stubborn woman, his mate. The sooner his wolf marked her and claimed her, the better. The smile disappeared as he thought about the words

Wren murmured in her sleep.

My enemy.

Had she sensed him, even in her sleep, and said it because of what happened at the gym, or was it due to some unrelated dream? Either way, he had to convince her that he was no foe—in love or business—if he wanted to keep her. He stared at the road ahead, knowing he could find no if in his heart when it came to hanging on to this woman. Wren was not just some bed slave captured in a raid—she was The One.

The thought of slaves sent his mind darting down a troubling path, one littered with Loki's past arguments. How many females, taken like Honoraria, had lived obediently under their master's command only to be felled by a primitive Viking tradition?

One supposedly cherished thrall had always accompanied a chieftain into the afterlife. After being passed from tent to tent, used by that chieftain's men in his honor, her throat was slit. Tender or brutal, their treatment of her up until that point made no difference. She was a thrall, a slave—her body was not her own. It was a vessel for the gift of life—precious seed passed along to the chieftain as the village watched him burn along with his favorite possession on the crackling funeral pyre.

No child he and Wren brought into the world would ever face such barbaric treatment. Odin himself wouldn't stop him from disemboweling any man who dared to threaten his daughter—and hanging his innards from a pole as a warning to others.

He pulled his vehicle into the driveway's entrance, gazing thoughtfully at the ferocious wolf in the center of the gate as it opened. You might want to tread lightly with the girl—and find space for your bar somewhere else. Would some other owner in the plaza be more interested in selling to him?

He would have his lawyer look into it.

The metal clanged shut behind him. He drove forward on a long U-shaped driveway shrouded in a multitude of trees. The woods provided more than shade—their home was a modern day fortress with a host of measures taken to keep out the prying eyes of the press.

He shut off the engine in the garage, looking over at the deceptively delicate beauty in his passenger seat. All the measures he and Loki had taken on the estate would serve a different purpose, now: Keeping someone in. His mate would remain locked away, safe and sound from outside influences until her rebellious heart and stubborn head understood why she was his precious to him.

Sliding Wren's fat leather purse over one shoulder—and grateful his brother wasn't there to see him carrying it—he deactivated the side door alarm. The woman was stronger than she looked. Her handbag weighed slightly less than a maiden's half-shield. After opening the door from the garage into the foyer, he carefully retrieved his sleeping prize.

Wren nuzzled against the skin of his neck with a soft sigh as he whispered, "Welcome home."

His cock hardened even more from the sound and the feel of her breath against his skin. He carried her over the threshold, smiling at the implication of the act, and struggled to discard the thought of dumping her on the couch, peeling the blue fabric from her bottom half, and exploring her pussy with his lips and tongue until she screamed for him.

Patience, not plundering, Gunnolf reminded himself.

He laid her down on the large black sofa long enough

to reset the alarm, push down the perpetually Wren-fueled erection in his pants, and whip out his cell phone. He sent a brief text to Loki, telling him that Wren was going to be a houseguest. His brother was curious, but Gunnolf kept it simple, leaving out any mention of the little woman's lineage. Some things they would need to discuss, later, in person.

He briefly debated placing Wren in a guest room. It would be the honorable thing to do. Then again, he'd sworn he was prepared to kill a female just a few days ago—that was already, by definition, entirely dishonorable, wasn't it?

Besides, Wren was going to be living here—she needed to get used to him. The sooner she did, the better off they would be. He settled on a happy medium between politeness and conquest, one that most certainly did not involve pretending that Wren's body belonged anywhere other than his room.

"They say a good relationship is built on honesty." He looked down at Wren's serene face, murmuring the words as he picked her up again and strode, down the hall, to the stairs leading up to his room, "I honestly want you naked in my bed. So that is the best place for us to begin."

CHAPTER FOURTEEN

Wren rolled over beneath an obscenely soft sheet. It must have had something like eight billion thread count. Fluffy goodness. She grunted and scratched the tip of her nose as a vaguely familiar scent rose from the pillow to greet her.

She yawned, flexing her fingers and toes. One arm stretched down, and the other reached over her head. Relaxed knuckles brushed against a pattern carved in thick wood. Her bed didn't have a headboard. Come to think of it, she rarely slept au naturel.

Uh-oh.

Keeping her eyes closed, she raised her arm, hesitantly feeling for the headboard, again. Yep. Still there, and she was still naked—stark raving nude, and starting to realize that the situational math wasn't adding up to anything good.

Where in the hell was she?

Less groggy and more worried, now, she cracked one eye—the blue one, for the record—open. Holding her breath, she performed an experimental side roll, checking out the opposite side of the mattress. There wasn't a body, but the dark sheet—and a black and gray comforter made from what her sweet, quasi-vegetarian heart sincerely hoped was faux fur—seemed like testosterone-inspired decor. Lurching into a seated position, she turned to consider the expensive slab of wood against the wall.

"Well, shit," she said, looking at a longboat with a billowing sail—like the one from her dream.

She once told Daisy Hell would freeze over before she ended up in another man's bed, but, surely, this didn't count. She hadn't signed up for this—she didn't even know what it was supposed to be.

Kidnapping? Abduction?

"This is not the time to panic," she reminded herself.

Battling a rush of adrenaline likely to give her a heart attack, she ran down a mental list of the various parts of her body: Hands untied. Feet untied. Back relaxed. Breasts okay. Butt fine. Vagina not sore at all. It was highly unlikely anything sexual had happened. Yet.

"Get you shit together, Wren," she said, glancing carefully at her surroundings.

Someone had shut the door to the room, so she had no idea who or what waited on the other side. Tightly closed drapes on the opposing wall blocked the view to what she hoped would be an escape route. A mechanical clock, with wavy symbols—runes, maybe—in place of traditional numbers, ticked softly nearby. The brass hands were in the right position for four-thirty. Assuming the time was correct, it was either early morning or late afternoon.

On the wall by the bed, she found a massive, colorful tapestry. It depicted a primitive waterside village in the shadow of a snow-capped mountain. There were lots of blondes. Across from it hung a wooden bookcase with shelves holding an eclectic assortment of books covering fitness, warfare, and philosophy. There was a smattering of fiction, too, but nothing else. Not a picture frame or a work badge in sight to confirm whose residence—snuff-film palace, rape house, chainsaw torture lodge, etc.—this was.

Past the table with two beveled glasses and a mighty fancy bottle of scotch, there was a bathroom door. A huge whirlpool bathtub waited beyond it—murder by bubble bath would probably be the least painful way for her to go, assuming the pervert was into peaceful deaths. Wren tried to remember anything about a guy approaching her, before or after yoga, but all she recalled was falling asleep under the old oak tree.

Had somebody drugged her water bottle? It wasn't typical behavior for the folks of Elation. It was extra crappy doing it to a free yoga instructor at a charity event. The only guy who had shown up for her sessions didn't seem like the type, at any rate. He might be okay with philosophy, but a soccer playing vegan pacifist with a man bun hairstyle wouldn't want the kind of image books on warfare would give him.

—Unless, of course, the man bun had been a lie.

"Well," she mumbled, forcing her limbs to move toward her captor's closet. Hopefully, it wasn't littered with lady-skin dresses or hipster clothes. "No sense in facing a debauched, lady mangling, bun wearing liar naked. That's just making the rest of his job way too easy."

Behind the door, she found a moth free walk-in with a multitude of hangers above a floor rack loaded with giant shoes. There were a few dress slacks, several long-sleeved shirts, and a plethora of t-shirts and jeans. All of it was of the Big and Tall variety, way too big for the man bun guy—as a matter of fact, only one person she had ever met was that size.

"Please, don't be who I think you are," Wren muttered.

Her heart did a backflip and a sideways rollercoaster drop into the pit of her stomach as she slid the nearest black t-shirt sideways off its plastic hanger. A brief memory of the woman and the white wolf leaped to mind as she slowly rotated the fabric so that the front, with its gold helmet and axes, faced her. There was no mistaking that logo or the last name, etched in big letters, on the front.

"God damn it," she said, her terror giving way to a righteous indignation. Even if he wasn't such a reputable businessperson, something told her the man was no serial killer. This kidnapping was part of some twisted intimidation tactic meant to bully her into selling her studio.

At least, now, she could rest one hundred percent easy on the no unconscious sex with Wren part. She was certain the meat-monster he kept locked up in the pairs of pants surrounding her would put her battery-operated boyfriend to shame—and she felt nothing, not even a twinge down there. Okay, technically, she did feel something, only it was more like a heartbeat centered in her clit—thump-thump, thump-thump—along with an obscene amount of moisture between her thighs at the thought of the man's undoubtedly generous cock.

"Dumbass," she told herself, "you should not be lusting after enemy meat."

Shooing away the thought, Wren lowered his shirt over her head. She pulled long hair out from underneath the back collar, shaking her head at the shameful intimacy of wearing her enemy's clothing. The soft material brushed possessively against her thighs with each step. Adding insult to injury, the drapes she yanked open revealed a sun-kissed view of her favorite lake through the locked door of a second-story balcony.

With her back turned on a view that she might have otherwise enjoyed, she strode for the only choice he had left her—the bedroom door. She opened it without hesitation, stepping out into the hallway, toward the stairs, with the man's business logo slapped across her chest like a made-to-order shipping label.

"Calm down," she said as the faint sound of classical piano—creepy, considering the guy's taste in music usually ran to people screaming about Asgaard—drifted up the stairs and down the hall. "Aside from not being naked, things are as bad as they're going to get."

CHAPTER FIFTEEN

"She will be impressed," Gunnolf assured himself, setting the final wine glass on the table. Consisting of grilled asparagus, salted turnip fries, and meticulously pepper-crusted flank steak, the robust two-person meal was definitely healthy and probably gourmet-level.

He wasn't all that fond of red wine, but the recipe book had promised it would make the best pairing, and even his hand-crafted centerpiece looked good. It was nice to have finally found a use for that crystal bowl. Filled with cheery sunflowers, lake stones, and water, it now made a suitable tribute for a water nymph—rather than forever remaining a useless housewarming gift that no one in their right minds should have given to two grown men.

Sensing she was awake, he grabbed the remote to the sound system, bumping Chopin down a few notches and listening for footsteps. Unlike the heavy metal he had recently used as a weapon against her, he figured she would find classical piano soothing.

Of course, he would need her to get over the whole Metal is noise attitude at some point—the honeymoon phase of their musical relationship could not last forever. He would also have to address the threat of which Loki had learned from her neighbor, along with her familiarity with self-defense. All of it could wait, for now, though—she was safe within these walls, and he wanted sex.

Seconds later, Wren wandered in from the hall, with the smooth skin of her legs peeking out from underneath one of his shirts. He had her panties in his pocket, so he knew she wore nothing underneath. It was a good look for her, although she would be even more beautiful with those bare legs wrapped around him. He watched as her expressive eyes flicked from his body to the table to the side door that led to the garage and back to him again.

"I am faster than you," he said, accurately reading the gesture. "Although, I would not mind the chase. And you should know all the windows and doors here have sensors."

"Kidnapping is a felony in the United States, you oversized Yeti," she answered flatly, crossing her arms in front of her chest.

"You mean oversized wolf," Gunnolf corrected her, his nostrils flaring as they picked up the scent of her arousal. She wanted to be here, with him, whether she was willing to admit it or not. "I am no snowman, and I am familiar with human law."

"I don't care what you think you are, you beef eating musclehead. You have to let me go."

"No." he pretended to ignore the insult, pulling out a chair for her. He was a beef eating musclehead? The scrape of chair legs on the floor seemed to grate on her nerves— good, she deserved it. "You are wrong. I do not have to let you go, nor do I intend to. Please, sit. Allow me to explain while we eat."

"Where are my clothes?" she asked.

The stubborn woman tapped her pink painted toes against the stone tiles. The expression beneath her bangs said she was not willing to listen or budge, not by an inch.

"Your stretchy things have been laundered and

tucked away in a safe place." Gunnolf crossed his arms as well. Fine. Until she stopped acting like a brat, he was not going to tell her about his brother's trip to her trailer and the closetful of clothes he had kindly retrieved. Or the vibrator Loki had seen on her bed and brought back to him—the one that was waiting patiently, in the top drawer of his bedside table, for a Gunnolf-guided reunion with her pussy.

"Give them to me," she demanded

"No," he replied.

"This is ridiculous! You can't bully me into signing over my business with your shady tactics."

"This is not about the studio, you stubborn woman." He was not asking nicely, this time, when he said, "Sit down."

"No."

"Because I am a reasonable man, I will give you a choice," he smiled pointedly, already knowing which thing he would prefer. "You can sit with me and eat the lovely meal I have prepared. Or I can carry you back upstairs, take that shirt off, and lick every inch of you until you're begging to be fucked. There's no point in denying you are turned on—I can smell it."

Gunnolf watched as Wren visibly flinched, clenched her jaw and slid into the chair he held out for her. Like the others, its back was in the shape of a shield. She scooted closer to the table, carefully avoiding contact with his hands. His wolf was willing to let it slide for now; she was there, and that was their first step. Besides, a ferocious spirit was preferable to a small woman cowering in tears. As long as she did not attempt to murder him, the rest should fall into place between them.

"I dislike meat," she said, skewering the steak with the tip of her fork before tearing into it viciously with the knife. "It's cruel."

"Ridiculous," Gunnolf responded, waving his own fork in the air at her, after swallowing a giant mouthful of the stuff. "You were meant to be a carnivore. Other animals are just a part of the food chain—and red meat is good for the iron in your blood. It prevents anemia."

"Last time I checked, you weren't my doctor—and he says my iron levels are just spiffy, thank you for asking," she answered in clipped tones after taking a careful sip of the red wine to wash down her last bite of asparagus.

"I am glad to hear you are in good health, but I still have my concerns about your diet." Gunnolf watched the small bites that she was taking from her plate with more than a little dismay.

"And I have my concerns about your having concerns that are none of your concern," Wren responded sarcastically, flipping her own fork in the air in Gunnolf's direction. "For the record, this whole psychotic holding me hostage deal of yours is not okay. Have you ever seen that movie with Foster and Hopkins, where the lambs shut up? If I were you, I'd be concerned about your mental health, not my eating habits, pal."

Gunnolf paused, closing his eyes for a moment to ask Freya for patience. His future mate was comparing him to a fictional man who ate people. Or did she mean the one who had made all those women put the lotion in the basket? Not that it mattered which serial killer it was—neither was acceptable. He had not intended to scare her in that way. Should he tell her the truth?

No, he could not fully explain what needed to happen just yet. The little beauty would likely launch under the table and stab him in the shins, or somewhere even worse, if he talked about her eating for two. It couldn't hurt to find out how she felt about marriage, though.

No, Freya cautioned inside his head, ask her about the wolves in her dream.

CHAPTER SIXTEEN

"Tell me about the wolves in your dream," Gunnolf demanded.

Wren dropped her fork. It landed in the midst of her turnip fries with an emphatic *clang*. How had he known? Had he planted the idea in her mind? Or maybe she was talking in her sleep, now. *Oh, God, no.* That would make her sex dreams super-awkward if she started calling out his name while he was listening.

His blue eyes regarded her intently, but the kidnapping bastard offered no further explanation. He just sat there, patiently, looking edible and waiting for her to speak.

Damn the man.

Big, sexy assholes like him were probably how Stockholm syndrome started in the first place. Dragging her mind away from the horrifying prospect of having that level of devotion to him, she thought about the golden-haired woman with the white wolf, instead.

More of the fairytale that had been eluding her came to mind: *Once upon a time, there was a lovely maiden, far away from home. She was lost, and tired, and wandering aimlessly atop a great mountain when she stumbled upon a giant wolf at rest in a clearing…*

She stared back at him and considered her circumstances. Gunnolf had laundered her things, put her to bed, and gone to the trouble of making a meal and setting the table. Why would he need to do any of those things? An evil man could just as easily have chained her up in his basement and attacked her while she was sleeping. But he hadn't done it. He also said this wasn't about forcing her to sell the studio.

So, what the hell did he want from her?

"I saw two wolves," Wren answered, her eyes shifting to contemplate the dining table. Seriously, did the man ever blink? "They were different colors. One was black, and one was white, but both had red eyes—and I heard the words *Viking* and *Berserker*."

"Is that all that happened?" he asked.

"No," she said.

"Tell me what else you saw," he prompted, in that sexy, Scandinavian baritone.

She had no idea why it interested him so much, but it was safer than going back to the *lick you all over* conversation.

"At first," she said, "I was in the water, by a village somewhere—only it wasn't me. I could see in my reflection that I was something *other* than human, and I was pregnant. The name Honoraria came to me."

"Honoraria," Gunnolf repeated. "Go on."

She looked up from the table for a moment. The way he had said the name, it held a ring of familiarity. His face seemed to think so, too.

"Then," she continued, considering a chip in the paint on her fingernails, "a ship came in. These horrible men poured from it in droves. Their eyes were red—inhuman— and they rowed to shore, howling. They were killing men and taking women, burning everything that they couldn't steal. I knew I had to help the villagers even though it meant endangering the baby."

"And this is when you saw the first wolf," he stated.

"Yes," Wren shuddered at the memory of the man's face even before he had turned into the animal. *That* had been the face of a man who intended to rape and degrade, to possess her like a plot of land or a piece of jewelry. "A man, with dark hair and a scar, appeared behind me. He leapt and turned into the dark wolf. I knew he was evil, and whatever innocence I had—that *Honoraria* had—would be destroyed by him."

"That man was my half-brother, Halvdan," Gunnolf's voice was quiet. "He was a special kind of werewolf—one who had been dead for many centuries."

Wren looked up, meeting his gaze across the table.

The idea was insane. If she accepted the things he was saying—that the world contained more than garden variety Homo sapiens and the events from her dream were real— then what she witnessed had taken place a long time ago. Not decades, but centuries.

"How old are you?" she asked.

"Ancient," he replied.

"How did Halvdan die?" she responded, toying idly with the food on her plate. As bizarre as it was to think of Gunnolf living forever, bossing people around for that amount of time would explain his unbelievable arrogance.

Explain it, but not excuse it, she reminded herself.

"Your ancestor, Honoraria, was a water nymph," he said, "She murdered Halvdan, not long after he made her his thrall, and fled. Thrall is the Viking term for a slave."

Your ancestor was a water nymph—did that mean Wren wasn't entirely human, either? That would be a valid reason for feeling crazy a third of the time, and sticking out like a square peg in a round hole in the orphanage, no matter how hard she had tried to fit in before Florence saved her.

She looked down at the fingers of her hands, spreading them wide and trying to imagine webbing between them as she asked, "Did you look for her—Honoraria?"

"I did more than look," he answered, gravely. "I hunted her across continents, but Honoraria always managed to stay one step ahead of me. The trail went cold—she may have died. Though I was following Odin's orders, Loki refused to participate. He claimed I was wrong, that it had been a matter of principle and what she did was justifiable—a mother saving her unborn child from slavery."

"And what did *you* say?"

"Murdering her master was a grave offense. Our family, our people, we lived by a code. Loki had always been the exception, playing the rebel and the fool," Gunnolf replied. He placed his big hands on the table and shrugged. It was a statement of fact, not an apology. "I do not imagine you will find it hard to believe that I was more … traditional and less forgiving?"

"No," she sighed—it was such an odd conversation to be having with him—but replied in all honesty. "You strike me as too proud for forgiveness."

"Then you already know me well." The admission came with a wry twist of his lips. "But I have interrupted your story, Wren, and that is not what I intended. Please, continue. What of the second wolf, the white one? Where did you see it and what did *it* do?"

She shifted uncomfortably in her chair. The cushion had worn thin beneath her bottom—a pertinent reminder of her predicament. She was sitting, nearly naked, across from, well, from whatever Gunnolf was supposed to mean to her.

Was he the man to whom she was attracted, or an

ancient being that had hunted her ancestor to the ends of the earth for vengeance? He could be one or the other, but he shouldn't be both.

"A lady in a cloak of feathers appeared, with the white wolf alongside her. She was the most beautiful woman I had ever seen, with long golden hair and a crown on her head."

"That was not just a woman that appeared to you. It was Odin's wife and partner, the goddess, Freya."

"How is that possible?" she asked. "I've never believed in that sort of thing."

"She believed in *you*," he answered, "and this mountain is very special—almost as special as you are. Freya asked Florence to save you. *That* is how you came to be adopted."

"How can you know that?" Wren questioned his statement. "You never met Florence."

"I did not know her," he agreed, "but a friend of hers recently sought me out, to explain the past. We will talk about it later. For now, tell me about the white wolf."

"There's not much to tell," she said. "Its eyes glowed red, the same as the black one's, and it stayed at Freya's side. I had a vision of it on the mast of another ship, and I was terrified—I *knew* it was my enemy, the same as the dark wolf, and that it would be coming for me."

"The black wolf was bad," Gunnolf frowned, shaking his head, "but the white one was never meant to be your enemy. Did Freya not attempt to explain any of this to you?"

"No," Wren answered. "She just looked sad and told me to sleep. She said when I woke up, we would begin to right all of the wrongs and finish my story."

CHAPTER SEVENTEEN

"No," Gunnolf growled. "She was supposed to tell you."

Righting wrongs sounded like a long, patient process. His wolf could not abide that—not when he already had Wren here, with her sweet scent so thick in the air. The wood on the section of the table he grabbed gave way with a resounding crack, something he felt guilty for when Wren jumped in her seat.

Swallowing hard at the redness that had surfaced in his eyes, she asked him, "What was Freya supposed to tell me, Gunnolf?"

He looked down at the ruptured wood, letting go with a frown. His mate was staring at him with widened eyes and he would have to replace a perfectly good dining table.

It was all Freya's fault.

"She should have told you. I am the white wolf." He tried hard to soften his tone for her, despite all the adrenaline coursing through his veins, "and there is no need for you to fear me because you are mine."

"What do you mean, I am yours?" Wren demanded of the wolf-man who had technically kidnapped her. "What makes me yours, Gunnolf?"

Look but don't touch, Gunnolf thought bitterly.

Freya was cruel—he could think of no other

explanation for dangling Wren in front of him this way. He might have expected that kind of thing from Odin, who would rather his wolf kill than keep her, but Odin hadn't talked to him in some time, and such fiendishness was beneath the goddess.

Speaking of beneath, he amended his thoughts with a lick of his lips, touching the tip of a protruding fang with his tongue. He and his barely leashed animal side both wanted her beneath them. Not just beneath them—above, beside, and all over them. Wren was here, in his home, wearing so little and smelling so good—there might never be a better opportunity.

"Claim her," his wolf said.

"I could never find Honoraria to kill her," Gunnolf growled, in agreement with his animal, as he came to his feet, "and Odin remained insistent over the centuries. There is a blood debt still owed for Halvdan's life. Freya, herself, has not changed his mind on the matter."

"Blood debt?" Wren squeaked. She made an obvious attempt to school her face and began pushing back from the table in increments. Her chair made tiny scraping sounds, and she talked to distract him from them. "Hold on a minute. I don't understand—are you telling me you want my blood?"

"It is your body I want, not just your blood," he assured her, his muscles coiling for the chase as he inched his way around the table. Though it had no intention of hurting her, his wolf was greatly looking forward to pursuit.

"Are you...?" Her legs rotated out from under the table—first one, then the other. She cleared her throat, her voice wobbling a bit as her eyes glanced at quite a few bites worth of well-seasoned meat left on the table. "Are you planning to eat me?"

Gunnolf's grin bared sharp, white teeth that were a little bit longer than they had been several minutes ago. He licked his lips, looking at the soft, creamy skin of her bare legs—so tasty—before answering. His voice dropped to an intimate rumble as he looked at the Y where those legs met and thought of the treasure to be pillaged between them.

"Oh, yes," he said.

Freya asked that he calm himself.

"No," The wolf inside of him immediately vetoed the goddess's suggestion.

Gunnolf handed over the reins to his animal, shooting around the table to reach for Wren. She would understand that she was in no danger soon enough.

"I am not dessert!" Wren shouted at the top of her lungs as she jumped to her feet, yanking her arm away. She tossed the plate with her leftovers—mostly meat and half-eaten turnip fries—at him before turning to run.

"Yes, you are," Gunnolf said.

He caught the plate against his chest, along with some food. The rest dropped to the floor at his feet. A flash of more leg, thanks to the hem of his t-shirt riding up as she dashed around the corner, made him smile as she fled down the hall, past the first set of stairs.

She most certainly was going to be his dessert—a delicious nymph candy that he fully intended to savor. He allowed her several seconds' worth of a head start. She wasn't reckless enough to hurt herself, and the alarm would sound the moment she breached the outside through a door or a window. Not that it would make a bit of difference. At this point, he knew that glorious scent of hers well enough to sniff it out in the midst of a crowded park full of cotton candy, hot dogs, and cheap beer.

"Ready or not; here I come!" Gunnolf roared as he

bounded down the hallway, his footsteps thundering like Thor's hammer in the narrowed space.

He inhaled deeply, following her intoxicating scent to a window. It remained locked, but his eyes picked up light scratches on the wood trim. Hopefully, she hadn't damaged her little pink fingernails.

He charged up the carpeted steps, taking two at a time. Wren had avoided the flight closest to the kitchen, which was also the nearest to his bedroom, on her way up. A good thing, since it gave her no choice but to head in that direction if she hoped to come back down without facing him.

The hallway was empty, but her heavenly scent was strong. There were plenty of open doors, and she hadn't been given enough time to reach the stairs. Whistling the opening notes of "Guardians of Asgaard"—one of the songs his little nymph had heard pounding through the walls of Fenric Fitness—he swaggered down the hall like a conquering hero.

He paused outside of the door to a guest bedroom that was just the slightest bit ajar, sniffing the air. Wren was there, on the opposite side of the wall. She must have been afraid that the slam of a door or even the click of its hardware would give her away.

A sliver of guilt stabbed at him while drumming his fingers on the entryway. Her breathing grew frantic as he stepped inside—she still didn't realize they were only playing a game. After a deliberate glance over at the curtains by the window, he dropped down on all fours to look under the bed.

Of course, she wasn't there—she was in the closet. The gesture was a courtesy, the gift of a few more seconds for her to recover. His tasty little treat was struggling to rediscover the dignity and calm that had gone to hell the instant she woke up naked in his room.

Gunnolf crossed the floor, placing his hand on the doorknob.

"I am opening the door, now," he rumbled. "Please believe that I would never seek to harm you, Wren. You are my mate. When I agreed that I wanted to eat you, I only meant your pussy—the thought of tasting you is driving me crazy."

CHAPTER EIGHTEEN

Wren slapped a hand over her mouth. She sank to her knees and peered through the small keyhole in the door, watching Gunnolf stride into the room as if on cue. She climbed to her feet quickly, scraping a knee in the process. Her heart refused to slow down—she was trapped, in a tiny closet, with the walls closing in on her.

Damn it.

The man was half animal—half wolf—and his eyes were red. Did that mean he was feral? He could move faster than anyone she had ever seen. A rock-solid table had cracked underneath those big hands of his—they would probably make quick work of her bones before he ate her. This whole situation was bad, so dreadfully, horribly bad.

Gods and blood debts were real, her dreams featured actual historical events, and a werewolf wanted to munch on her. Shit. Two sandwiches shy of a picnic, that's what her brain was—and she was hugging herself in a straightjacket, somewhere, thinking it was actually this closet. She couldn't even talk her stupid panty-free pussy out of its irrational juiciness for a man who had clearly stated that he was going to dig into her like an ice cream sundae.

If that didn't spell nuts, nothing did.

"I am opening the door now," he rumbled from the opposite side of the closet. "Please believe that I would never seek to harm you, Wren. You are my mate. When I agreed that I wanted to eat you, I only meant your pussy—the thought of tasting you has been driving me crazy."

Wren gripped the wood on the inside of the doorframe as he gently opened the door. She had to because her knees were threatening to buckle. All he wanted to eat was her pussy? Her inner walls clenched at the idea of his mouth down there. Something told her he was going to do an excellent job, although the thought of him having lots of experience at it came with an irrational pang of jealousy.

"Listen," she said, leaning hard into the frame as she looked up into a pair of obscenely gorgeous blue eyes. "I still have way too many questions about what's going on here, especially this whole I'm your mate thing."

"Okay," he answered nicely, pulling her hands away from the wood and grabbing her by the waist. "After I finish my dessert, we can talk."

A pair of impossibly thick arms lifted her against his chest, carrying her effortlessly out and down the hall, toward the room where she had awakened. Gentle as he was, she knew he wouldn't let her escape. Hell, she wasn't sure she wanted to, anymore. Her mind added on to the fairytale of its own volition:

Once upon a time, there was a lovely maiden, far away from home. She was lost, and tired, and wandering aimlessly atop a great mountain when she stumbled upon a giant wolf at rest in a clearing. It kidnapped her and ate her pussy like nobody's business. The End.

"No," she said, as they entered the Viking's bedroom. There had to be more to the story than mind-shattering oral pleasure. As a matter of fact, the tale had been related to her during childhood so there shouldn't have been any sex in it at all.

"Why do you tell me no?" He countered, "I promise

you, mit hjerte —you will enjoy it."

"Sorry." She responded, wondering what meet yatta—at least, that's what the words sounded like—meant and having no doubt he could make her vagina incredibly happy. "I wasn't talking to you."

He looked around in frustration, "Did Freya say something to you? If she tries to dissuade you from sex, do not listen. "

"Freya?" She frowned at him. "No, she didn't say anything. What did you just call me?"

"Mit hjerte—my heart," he answered matter-of-factly. "Whose voice did you hear, then? Was it Odin's? Is he threatening you?"

"Oh, for..." Wren winced, realizing how bad her confession was going to sound. "It wasn't Odin. Sometimes I talk to myself. Out loud. Alright?"

"I can live with that," Gunnolf shrugged, placing her on her back at the edge of the furry comforter and kneeling on the floor between her legs.

He slowly feathered his hands along the bottoms of her feet before moving on to her ankles and shins. His fingers were long and slightly calloused, the coarseness of their tips coaxing goose bumps from her as he worked his way up. By the time his head bent to tenderly kissed the scratches on her right knee, she was trembling. Anywhere and everywhere the man touched her felt heavenly.

She propped herself up on her elbows watching in fascination as his hands splayed over her thighs, stroking and massaging them. The look he gave her when their eyes met bordered on the depraved.

"Take off the shirt, mit hjerte," he commanded, teasing the delicate skin on the inside of her thigh. A solitary finger moved back and forth within inches of the V where her legs met. "I will not lick this pretty pussy and make you cum until you show me that beautiful body of yours."

She shivered, remembering her fantasy—the feel his thick fingers filling and stretching her. His eyes were bright red, and the corner of one fang peeked out from beneath his top lip as she sat all the way up for him. God, he was sexy, like this, dangerous and sexy—and he thought she was beautiful.

Our mate, a new voice whispered inside of her. She hadn't been certain what this mate thing entailed when he'd said it before, but something inside of her was waking up just for him. It was waking up, and her body was telling her, in no uncertain terms, that mate meant sex.

Thank God.

She gripped the hem of his t-shirt, pulled it over her shoulders and dropped it beside her on the bed as his hands skimmed her hips and torso. Sex was A-OK. No, where this man was concerned, sex was spectacular. It was all the other crap—commitment and whatnot—that her heart couldn't handle.

CHAPTER NINETEEN

Gunnolf held his breath as Wren sat up, pulling his t-shirt over her head. Her eyes glowed with magic—the nymph inside of her was coming out to play with his wolf, and she was beautiful. He had promised to take care of her pussy, and he would, but there was something else he wanted to do, first, something he'd been dying to do ever since he'd set eyes on her.

His fingers skimmed the soft skin of her hips and the outside of her ribs, reaching for the swell of her breasts as she dropped the shirt. They were even more exquisite than he remembered. He wondered if he could get away with a "no clothing for Wren indoors" house rule—Loki certainly wasn't likely to mind the view.

Then again, he might have to strangle his brother for looking.

He rose from the floor swiftly, brushing her lips with his own as he moved into a seated position beside her. She moaned when his tongue slid into the cavern of her mouth, invading and exploring her sweetness. His hands cupped the firm little globes he'd been dreaming about since he first saw hints of them outside his gym. Squeezing lightly, he swirled his thumbs around the areolas, enjoying the way they tightened and changed with her excitement. He pulled away and looked down into her eyes as he strummed the big pink nipples begging for his attention in the center.

"You are mine," he told her. "My treasure."

"I'm beginning to see," she responded, moving to straddle his lap, placing a leg on either side of his jeans as she arched her back, thrusting her breasts out for closer inspection, "that you're not too shabby, yourself."

"So responsive," he growled, rolling a nipple between his thumb and forefinger as he scraped the other with his teeth, then laved it with a gentle tongue. "You like having these pretty tits played with, don't you?"

"Yes," she gasped as he gave the other nipple the same treatment.

"It makes that sweet little pussy even wetter, doesn't it?" Threading one hand in the back of her hair, he pulled her close and growled the words in her ear. The other hand moved in between them as he used his legs to spread her own wider apart.

"It does," she sighed into his neck, obviously enjoying the rough feel of the denim beneath her naked skin as he slid the tip of a thick middle finger inside of her. A second soon joined it.

Gunnolf licked at the shell of her ear, holding her head in place as he slid the invading digits deeper, gently pumping them in and out between the slick walls now sheathing them. He chuckled at the way she jumped when his thumb found her clit and began to work it in time with the movement of his finger.

"You want to cum for me already, hmm?" He knew how she felt—his cock was so hard it hurt. "Before I even put my mouth on that luscious cunt."

"Ah," She shuddered and struggled for words as his calloused thumb worked at the overly sensitized bundle of nerves. "I ... yes."

"I will let you, eventually," he answered, sliding his

fingers out and his hand away from her pussy. He let go of her neck so she could raise her head and look into his eyes.

"Why not now?" she frowned back at him, her face flushed. She was practically squirming.

"Because I am the one in control—my room, my rules, " he winked back at her, licking her juices from his finger before sliding his tongue into her mouth so that she could taste them, too. The stubborn woman seemed frustrated with him and herself, which told him it was probably part of some fantasy—only, now that he was doing it, the power play pissed her off.

She stared back at him in disbelief as he picked her up off his lap, placing her into her previous position, on her back, on the bed.

"Besides," he said, ignoring his wolf's protests as he stood, breaking away from her to pull the food-smudged shirt he wore over his head, "you hardly seemed grateful for all my hard work. You did not say thank you, threw a plate at me, and dumped the meal I prepared for you all over the floor."

"Are you seriously accusing me of rudeness at a time like this?" she asked him, her tone growing defensive as she popped up into a seated position.

"I have accused you of nothing," he fought the urge to smile, towering over her with his hands on his denim-clad hips. "I merely described your actions. You are the one who came to the conclusion it was rude."

"I..." she paused, "but I want an orgasm."

"Welcome to my world," he responded wryly, raising his eyebrows.

"Oh," Wren blushed. Her fingers found the zipper on his jeans—quid pro quo sounded more reasonable to her. "Well, what if I told you how sorry I was?"

"I would say," he answered, helping her push the jeans and boxers from his legs, "that words minus actions mean little."

Her eyes widened at the length of his cock as it sprang free. It bobbed proudly before her eyes, growing even more from the attention. She licked her lips and wrapped a hand around it, pumping tentatively.

He groaned as her soft hand engulfed his hot flesh. His wolf urged him to stop playing, to toss her back onto the bed, ram their dick into her pussy and their fangs into her shoulder—mark their mate, claim her as theirs forever. NOW. He told it no. He would not rush these priceless moments. It was their first time with Wren—their beautiful mate was just getting used to them, and they were just beginning to discover and explore her.

"It's official," she mused, climbing to her knees on the mattress and dipping her head down to lick tentatively at the moisture seeping from the slit at the top, "you're a big boy all over."

"Big, yes," he replied, watching her savor the taste of him, "but I am no boy. I was raiding monasteries long before the gods ever dreamed of your existence, woman."

"Semantics," she answered, boldly wrapping her lips around his cock. She bobbed her head, sucking at it hungrily for a bit before freeing her mouth with a loud, wet pop and a wicked smile. "Wouldn't you agree?"

"I would," he rumbled, feathering a gentle hand through her hair. He was glad to see her so comfortable with him—and so eagerly welcoming his dick inside that plump, slick mouth of hers. "When we are naked together, you can call me whatever you like."

CHAPTER TWENTY

Wren licked her lips and looked up into his eyes. She couldn't deny some hand, whether Freya's or Santa Claus was at work here. Having met Gunnolf barely two days ago, here she was, naked and wanton, with his shaft in her hand and the warm salty taste of him fresh on her tongue. There was no denying something inside of her responded to his wolf—it had called him mate. Too bad none of this sexiness between them negated his talk about Odin and blood.

"In the other room," she said, stroking her fingers up and down his cock, enjoying her control and his response to it, "you told me you would never seek to harm me."

"That is true," he smiled down at her, "because you are my mate—you feel it, too, don't you?"

"Yes," she responded with a nod—no point in denying what the man did to her hormones, "but what about this debt for Halvdan. Don't you need my blood?"

"No," he answered carefully, "there is another way, thanks to Freya."

"What is that?" She wondered why he hadn't mentioned it in the first place.

He searched her eyes for a moment.

"What is the other way, Gunnolf?" she asked him again.

"A child," he answered.

"No," she frowned—the idea chilled her blood.

"There is no way I am letting you harm a child."

"That is not what I meant," he assured her, running a thumb over her bottom lip.

"Then tell me what you did mean," she demanded as he bent down.

"I will tell you," he murmured against her lips, "once you are on your back, with your legs spread wide so I can taste that pretty pussy, mit hjerte."

"No," she glared back at him, certain he was stalling on the topic of him murdering some toddler or teenager to save her life. "You tell me now."

"No," he responded just as adamantly. "Has no one ever told you keeping a Berserker Wolf from what he wants is dangerous? If you wish me to speak on the matter, lie down, first."

She rolled her eyes and hit him with a heavy dose of sarcasm. "Considering no one in my gigantic social circle even knew that they were real? Yeah, that would be a big fat N-O, Fang Boy."

"Do not roll your eyes at me," he warned.

"Do not ask me stupid questions," she responded, a bit surprised the stubborn man hadn't challenged the nickname. Note to self: He hadn't been kidding when he said she could call him whatever she liked while they were naked.

"Down," he commanded, "now."

"Talk," she defied him, crossing her arms, "now."

He wrapped a thick arm around her waist, ignoring her indignant gasp as he lifted her. The other hand unfolded her legs, gently but firmly, from beneath her so that he could work on getting them in the position he desired at the foot of the bed.

"No one has ever accused me of having patience," he

offered while reaching over her head to grab a pillow.

It was an inadequate means of apology.

"I'm shocked," she responded dryly.

He chose to ignore the rejoinder, positioning the pillow under her butt and her heels up on the edge of the bed. Lowering his head, he pressed a palm on the inside of either thigh to ensure they stayed open while he dropped his head down, tickling her abdomen with his breath.

"From this moment forward," he spoke authoritatively, raising his head just enough to make eye contact, "we operate by my rules. You will agree to entrust me, entirely, with your body and your pleasure—which means you will only cum when I say you can."

Wren's heart sped up at the chill of the air on her pussy. They were back to her fantasy again. Entrust him with her pleasure. Could sex honestly be that simple? Steven hadn't thought so. He said he hated going down on her, that women were disgusting down there. The only other man to ever inspect her was Dr. Lazlo, and only because he was paid to do it. Did Gunnolf truly want to, or was he just making a sacrifice for her benefit?

"You don't have to do it." She licked her lips, hating the insecurity in her voice as she started over, "I mean, I've only had one other partner before you, and he didn't..."

"Two," he corrected her matter-of-factly.

"No," she responded adamantly, "I have not. If anyone other than Steven is claiming it, they're lying."

"Not another man," he answered. "A sex toy."

"Oh, well, yes," she frowned. How did the man know about that? "If you count Mongo, I guess that makes two partners. Either way, I'm not used to that, so, you know, you don't have to feel obligated to do something if you don't want to."

His lips brushed her belly button in a soft kiss, the slick thrust of his tongue dipping into it before he looked up at her.

"Aside from your musical prejudice, you are perfect," he assured her in a voice that turned her insides to gelatin. "I have thought of doing little else, aside from this, since I first met you."

See, she reasoned with herself as she lay down, his mouth flicking and caressing a slow path down to her smooth mons. It's fine. There was no harm in letting the sexy beast have his way with her, first, before they talked, right? It wasn't like he had some doppelgänger he dispatched to murder people while he was busy doing delightfully dirty things to women.

Did he?

"Wait," she sat up again. "Berserker Wolves don't have evil twins, do they?"

He muttered something—she assumed it was an expletive—and nipped at the inside of her thigh. It was just enough to ensure that she felt the reprisal.

"No, mit hjerte," he said. "There is no evil twin. If there were, he would be here, right beside you, keeping that beautiful mouth of yours too busy to ask ridiculous questions."

She frowned down at him, prepared to say something rude. He must've known because a stream of air blown directly onto her exposed clit preempted the thought. He followed up with a warm mouth and swirling tongue that teased her, ramping her up to the precipice of an orgasm and backing off when she grabbed at his hair and arched her hips in desperation.

"Please," she whimpered.

"Perhaps you should ask my evil twin," Gunnolf

chuckled, moving down to lap at her honeyed slit from bottom to top, instead.

"You are the evil one," she groaned in answer.

He didn't disagree. Instead, he drew broad, teasing patterns against the slick, swollen folds of her outer labia with a firm tongue. She panted and writhed, incoherent with need by the time he swiped her sensitive inner lips.

"Damn you," she said, her legs melting as his tongue probed her center, plunging inward, "please."

CHAPTER TWENTY-ONE

Mine, his wolf growled possessively as his tongue dove inside her quivering channel. The smell of Wren, the taste of her was ambrosia. He would need to bite her soon, marking her permanently to cement the bond that Freya had predestined in the eyes of the rest of the Supernatural world.

The only question was whether he should do so before of after explaining the need for offspring.

He replaced his tongue with a finger, pumping it gently in and out and adding a second, soon after. Scattering delicate butterfly kisses, ever so lightly, across her mons, he used his lips to draft a roadmap of desire.

"Now," he flicked a moistened tongue against the skin his mouth had been caressing, asking her, "Would you like to cum for me, mit hjerte?"

"Yes," she shuddered in reply, her pupils dilating.

"Good girl," he responded.

"Woman," she managed to gasp as his tongue found the bundle of nerves for which it had been searching.

"Good woman," he echoed, not bothering to look up from where his thumb pressed the skin of her pubic mound upward, exposing the lovely pink button for him.

He could have argued that, compared to the numerous lives he had experienced, she was a girl. Just about all of the women he had known would have taken the term as a compliment, had they even considered it, at all.

Then again, she was the daughter of a giant-slayer and the only female he had ever encountered who did not believe her tears a tool for emotional blackmail.

Besides, arguments served no valid purpose among naked, sexy people.

He plunged his fingers in and out of her honeyed opening, angling them to rub at the small patch of spongy flesh running along the inside wall of her pelvis. His tongue flicked relentlessly at her clitoris as she thrashed and moaned for him. Plying her secret spot in tandem, he sent her spiraling closer and closer to that final point, where she surrendered her will and her nerve-endings exploded in a rush of sensation.

When he knew she was almost there, he commanded, "Cum for me, now—say my name."

She gasped and thrashed at the intensity of the sensations crashing over her. Her body gave in to the inevitable spasms, but her mouth sent a different message, loud and clear.

She shouted asshole in place of his name.

"That," Gunnolf raised his head, along with an eyebrow, more amused with her than angry as he spoke, "is not my name, mit hjerte."

"That," she rasped the words, rolling her head to one side and waving a boneless hand in the air at him, "is a matter of opinion."

So, she was back to insulting him again, like she had when she was standing outside of his door at the gym. He pressed a kiss to the sweat-drenched skin over one hipbone and chuckled, "You are a saucy little thing—I like that."

"Saucy?" she grumbled. "You make me sound like a packet of gravy."

"One I would gladly pour all over me," he responded,

wagging his eyebrows and looming over her as he bracketed her body between his hands on the bed.

"No," she said, firmly, while slapping at his forearms because she wasn't strong enough to move them on her own. "You just got what you asked for—there will be no more pouring until you explain this whole Freya-child thing."

"Just one kiss," he insisted.

"You're not getting a kiss."

"Yes, I am."

"You just had your mouth all over my vagina," she said. "Why in the hell is a kiss such a big deal?"

"Because you don't want me to have it," he smiled, easing down into the bottom of a push-up to brush his lips against hers. He hovered over her with ease, taking his time as he snaked his tongue into the warmth of her mouth to parry with her own. After finishing, he gave her a peck on the cheek and said, "And because you need to know how delicious you are."

"You have serious issues," she answered, grabbing for the discarded t-shirt, in the name of modesty, once he'd rolled off her.

"As do you," he countered, watching her cover up but refusing to do the same. "We were made for each other."

"Less stalling, more talking," she said, scooting all the way up to the wooden headboard.

"You make me smile," he rolled over onto his belly, hiding his stiff cock in the mattress as he kicked his feet up in the air like a twelve-year-old girl at a slumber party. Grabbing one of Wren's feet—the toes on it were so delicate and cute with their tasteful pink polish—he made one final effort at distraction, pressing his thumbs into her sole in a sensual, circular motion.

"I never smile," he added.

"Issues," she repeated, kicking at his hand.

Gunnolf sighed, propping his elbows on the bed and his chin on his fists as he looked up at her. It had been a mistake mentioning Freya's plan so early. He had yet to set dick into the Promised Land, and a woman like Wren was not likely to consider the prospect of birthing a child for him foreplay.

You did this to yourself, Freya whispered. I told you to wait.

Wren's eyes widened when his wolf growled at the goddess's complaint.

"What was that?" Wren demanded

"My wolf," he frowned, assuming she thought he had growled at her when he had not.

"Your wolf is female?"

"My..." he sat up on the bed. "No, he is not. You heard Freya?"

"If that's who it was, then, yes," she responded. "What did she mean by she told you to wait?"

He paused for a moment, considering things. He had not left a mark on her skin yet, or deposited his seed between those lovely, limber thighs. Regardless, she heard the voice in his head. Maybe the mating bond was already falling into place?

She should not have heard me. Freya sounded perturbed. I had not intended it.

"Well, your intentions be damned, I can hear you," Wren responded, "and it's creepy, you talking about me like I wasn't here, so...oh, my GOD, you were watching us the whole time, weren't you?"

There is nothing to be ashamed of, my child, Freya responded. Your bodies are beautiful, and love is my domain.

"I am not your child—I am also not some peep show," Wren said, drawing her knees up into her chest, stretching the t-shirt down to cover everything but the tips of her toes.

"My Lady," Gunnolf spoke to Freya, his voice incredibly polite. "While I realize you have our best interests at heart, here, I believe it is best to allow us to speak in private."

Fine, Freya answered. I will leave the two of you in peace from now on. And it will be up to you to thoroughly explain, on your own, the need to impregnate her.

CHAPTER TWENTY-TWO

"Impregnate me?" Wren shrieked, tightening her arms protectively around her knees and wishing for a chastity belt. "No, no, no, NO. I am not the Mommy type. Even if I were, you just met me. In what deluded universe did you and your perverted goddess think that would possibly be okay?"

"It is our destiny. Why else would you feel so drawn to me?" Gunnolf responded, scooting closer to brush his fingers gently over her cheek.

"Have you looked in the mirror recently?" she answered sarcastically, pushing his hand away.

"Yes," he smirked, flexing his muscles to prove the point, "but it is more than that—it is fate. In this world or any other, you are meant to be mine."

"Hold on, Captain Conceited," she glared at the obscenely handsome man, "I thought that mates were just an intense fuck buddy thing."

"Then, you were mistaken," he answered, ruffling her bangs. "We are meant to spend the rest of our days in each other's arms."

Once upon a time, a sarcastic voice in her head drowned out the one agreeing with him, there was a lovely maiden far away from home. She was lost, and tired, and wandering aimlessly atop a great mountain when she stumbled upon a giant wolf at rest in a clearing. It kidnapped her, basted her uterus in wolf baby juice, and dropped her like a hormonal hot potato.

"Yeah, right," she snorted, "says the man wanting to use me as a donation cup at the local sperm bank. That's probably what some horny asshole told my biological mother nine months before she abandoned me on the doorstep of that sadistic orphanage."

He growled, his fangs extending at the thought of anyone hurting her as an adorable, wide-eyed child.

Unfortunately, she took it the wrong way and flinched.

"I would never hurt you," he sighed.

"Good," she answered, sliding her legs off the side of the bed in a disturbingly cheery manor, "then you can let me go."

"No." He jumped to his feet in a blur, taking a seat against the headboard and pulling her onto his lap along with him. "I cannot do that either."

"Yes, you can," she argued, wriggling on his lap as she attempted to remove the arm clamped around her waist. It was like trying to move the foundation of a building.

"Ask anybody—I'm super easy to abandon."

"Not for me." He placed a kiss on the top of her head. "I will never let you go. Ever. Let me tell you a story, instead."

She sighed, falling still against him once she realized what her frantic movements had been doing for the raging erection now twitching against her bottom.

"It doesn't start with once upon a time, does it?" she asked. "Because I'm getting a little sick of that one."

"No," he laughed, a booming, happy sound, as he stroked her hair. "This is something that a fox named Sylvie told me."

"Sylvie?" she asked, cocking her head toward the soothing motions of his hand. Damn his wolfy ass. Even that felt amazing. "You mean the not-so-natural redhead that spoke to me at Florence's memorial service?"

"The same one," he answered. "She knew your adoptive mother for quite some time before you came along."

"How is that even possible?" she began, trying to turn and face him.

"Hush," he answered, holding her still, "and I will tell you."

There he went, again, trying to be the boss of her.

Gunnolf went on to explain that Florence had once been an elf, probably nearly as old as he and Loki. She had been beautiful, immortal, and strong—a giant slayer. She and Sylvie had been very close, possibly mated, before the goddess Freya came to tell Florence about a lovable little girl, with one blue eye and one green one, locked away in an evil orphanage.

This girl was part of a nymph (Honoraria)'s bloodline unfairly cursed by Freya's husband, Odin, after said nymph killed one of his Berserker Wolves (Halvdan). Odin's wife, never fully agreeing with her husband on anything because she was a stubborn female, had decided to create a loophole capable of both thwarting and satisfying Odin's will someday. Technically, because of how fate worked, she had to ask the three Norns—females steering the course of destiny from the Well of Urn—to do it for her.

"Are you saying...?" Wren stopped his hand, driven by a burning curiosity. She was cool with Florence being a lesbian. As a matter of fact, looking back, it made sense. But why on earth would any higher power deem her important enough to be a loophole?

"What I am saying, at the moment, is nothing," he scolded, nipping gently at her fingertips, "because you are a naughty woman who has interrupted my highly entertaining tale."

"Fine," she grumbled, although she was rather enjoying the story. "Go ahead."

Hugging her tightly, he picked up the tale with what Freya told the elf. There was a way to alleviate the suffering of this precious child, but it involved a favor of sorts—an enormous sacrifice from a loving heart. If Florence were willing to give up her immortality, to live out a finite number of days, growing old, fate would allow her to adopt the child and give her happiness no other descendant had ever known.

"So Florence gave up everything for me," Wren finished, sadly.

"According to Sylvie, Florence never regretted it," he answered. "Why would she, when she got to be the mother of an extraordinary little girl? You are the loophole she fell in love with, and you have bloomed into a remarkable woman—one that Freya, the Norns, and the entire universe—aside from Odin—intended for me to find and love."

She sighed, leaning back against him and rubbing at an eyebrow.

"Do you understand now?" he asked her.

Wren thought, again, of the story she'd been struggling to remember since she met him:

Once upon a time, there was a lovely maiden far away from home. She was lost, and tired, and wandering aimlessly atop a great mountain when she stumbled upon a giant wolf at rest in a clearing...

"I think so," she answered. "You're saying this whole

mate thing means you're my once upon a time, and the universe devised the story. So, all that's left for us to do is get me pregnant—we create a new life, Freya outsmarts Odin, I get to live, and voilà! The debt is satisfied.

"Yes," he nodded.

"Well, that's too fucking bad," she said, smacking his arm, "I hate to burst your bubble, but this is one gal that doesn't do babies. And don't you dare say a single word about my age and some imaginary biological clock or, so help me God, I will stab you right in the eye with a fingernail."

CHAPTER TWENTY-THREE

"But," Gunnolf said, dropping the arm that had been holding her, dumbfounded—apparently, some women didn't love babies. "The only alternative…"

"Is a flaw in your thinking," Wren challenged. She slid out of his reach and onto the floor, walking over to his bookshelf. "According to Odin, there were zero alternatives. Now, Freya says there is one. Maybe the Norns aren't that fond of the gods telling them what to do, and our lives are more flexible than you believe."

"What you are saying, right now, this is not a good thing, mit hjerte," he pleaded, sliding into his boxers. The only alternative was a flaw in his thinking? He was going to have to remove The Art of War from his shelf and hide it from her. "You must not defy the gods. I swear I will never abandon you, and pregnancy is such a small price to pay for safety and long-term happiness."

"Sure. It's a small price for someone who won't be losing control of his body for nine months. Or sweating for umpteen hours, squeezing a gargantuan wolf baby through an orifice that, width wise, is smaller than the holes on a golf course," she responded, tossing the heated words over her shoulder.

"But you will always be beautiful to me, " he said, stepping up behind her to place his hands on her shoulders. It was a blind attempt at reassurance—but he wasn't above trying it at this point. "Especially in childbirth."

"Are you deaf and stupid?" She spun around, smacking him in the chest. "I am talking about pain, not vanity."

"Is that all that you are worried about?" he chuckled, suddenly relieved. "It will not be like that, at all. It will be a beautiful experience—you will be my beloved mate, bringing our child into the world."

"Sorry," she said, pushing him away from her, "I'm not buying into all that hopeless romantic bullshit. Daze already debunked the wonders of childbirth for me."

"Who is Daze?" he demanded. The name didn't sound familiar, and he needed to know the identity of the person poisoning his mate's mind so he could keep Wren away from her.

"Who is Daze?" Wren repeated, mocking his tone, with her hands on her hips. "Daze is Daisy, my best friend in the world—who has known me a lot longer than you and given birth three times. Plus, a bona fide giant slayer raised me. I'm telling you, right now, I don't care if the cost of freedom is high—it's better than surrender or submission."

"Stubborn, crazy woman," he growled, in silent agreement with his wolf that they should have just mounted her earlier and gotten it over with, "I have no idea what you are talking about."

"She was paraphrasing JFK as a means to summarize her liberation from the oppression of gods and men," Loki interjected from the open doorway, a broad grin painted on his face. "Also, possibly offering us sex of the protected variety in exchange for teaching her how to fight whatever Odin sends her way. Does that sound about right, little birdie?"

Gunnolf could have gladly strangled his brother for

his tone and the way that he leaned in the doorway and winked at Wren. Of course, the charismatic little bastard would know whom she was quoting—and she was not offering Loki anything, damn it.

Wren's neck whipped around in the direction of the doorway, a blush staining her cheeks. She told Loki that yes, it was JFK, and asked how long he'd been standing there.

"A minute or two," Loki responded off-handedly, "but I have been in the house the whole time. Our sense of smell is not the only thing that is exceptional about shifters—our hearing is top notch, too. You make the sweetest sounds when someone is giving you pleasure, but, between you and me, my favorite part is where you called my big brother an asshole."

"I was taught by a wise woman not to mince my words," she answered wryly, glancing at the jealous expression on Gunnolf's face with something close to disgust. "And your sibling here wants me to believe my only alternative to death is letting him use my womb like some baby baking convection oven for Freya the Almighty."

Gunnolf flinched at her assessment. Was that truly what his little mate thought? She made it sound so clinical and cold—as if they were discussing the prospect of some lab experiment, rather than the act of building a family together.

"The old will of the gods speech, eh?" Loki laughed. "I have been battling that mentality for centuries. You are a wise woman not to enable him—my therapist says he is a control freak. And I think teaching you to fight is a stellar idea. Has he told you about the death threat painted on your mailbox yet?"

"The what?" she responded, her jaw dropping.

"I was waiting for the right time," Gunnolf growled,

walking over to his closet and yanking open the door. He was certain his eyes glowed red again, and he could feel the tip of his fangs poking into the meat of his top lip—his wolf was dying to teach his brother's some respect.

On the other hand, he was grateful to find some of Wren's clothes draped over hangers inside. Loki must have snuck in while they were eating—it was the second decent decision Loki had made, after enlisting Sylvie's help to drop off Wren's car. He slid a pair of tiny stonewashed jeans from one of the plastic frames and placed the denim squarely in his mate's hands.

"Cover yourself," he demanded, gripping her shoulders to steer her in the direction of the bathroom.

"But I don't have any panties," she complained through the closed door.

"You do not need them," he said—there was no way he was giving up the ones in his pocket. He turned to Loki and hissed, "You are making me look bad in front of my mate."

"Nope," Loki responded. "You are doing that all on your own, bro."

Gunnolf raised his eyebrows at the language and responded, "How many times must we have this discussion? Respectable businessmen do not use slang—ever."

"The term is businesspeople, businessmen is considered sexist—and whatever, bro," Loki answering loudly, his eyes twinkling as Wren snickered in response, over the rustling of clothes on the opposite side of the door. "I am going downstairs to finish cleaning up the disgusting mess from your juvenile food fight. Once the little birdie and you are fully dressed, you might want to join me downstairs. We need to discuss any enemies Wren might have, and hammer out the details of a training schedule."

CHAPTER TWENTY-FOUR

"Die, bitch," Wren repeated, staring at the two brothers sitting across from her—both handsome in their own right, though Gunnolf was the best-looking—at the cracked dining room table. "Are you serious?"

"Loki may be a fool," Gunnolf said, with a sideways glance at his younger sibling, "but he is no liar."

Loki rolled his eyes, the blue of them so similar to his brother's as he told her, "You just met the man—I've been putting up with this my whole life."

She laughed in spite of herself, mostly due to the murderous look on her mate's face. No, not mate—mates got people pregnant.

He awakened your magic, the voice inside of her insisted.

Great, she responded silently, not even sure what awakening her magic meant, but that doesn't mean I owe him a baby.

"Is there anyone you can think of that might wish you dead?" Loki probed.

"No," she responded, "Steven is the only person I know that might want to hurt me. Even if he were still in town, he wouldn't do something like this. Beat me up and steal from me, yes, but a death threat isn't his style."

Gunnolf, clenched his jaw and drummed his fingers on the wood, calming himself before asking, "Have you done anything recently that might anger someone to a murderous level, even a stranger?"

"Doubtful," she frowned, her eyes drawn by the crystal bowl, with its sunshine-colored flowers, in the center of the table. "I donated some things to the women's shelter, along with my time for the yoga event, but I doubt that's important."

"Probably not," Loki agreed. "Is there anything else, anything at all that stands out to you?"

"Well," she licked her lips, staring at the smooth stones beneath the petals. "Daisy was doing some research for me—trying to find anyone who might know something about my birth mother. She has contact information for a woman who worked in the orphanage before it burned."

"The orphanage where Florence found you, it burned down?" Gunnolf clarified.

"Uh-huh," she said, still distracted by the gray and white pebbles—was she crazy, or had she felt a connection to them? "It happened not long after I was adopted."

She flexed an empty hand experimentally, imagining the rocks were in her palm. Weird. She could feel them—they were cool and damp, bearing an echo of the lake that had shaped them over time.

Gunnolf nodded and rumbled, "From what Florence shared with Sylvie, it was not a nice place for a child. Perhaps this fire was an act of arson, not an accident. This woman your friend found might have set it."

"Or she could have something else to hide," Loki commented, steeling his fingers. "Can you tell us what you remember about this place?"

"There's not a lot," Wren sighed, disconnecting from the small stones. She rubbed the back of her neck. That place was hell—she had been blocking out most of the memories for years. "They were cruel to me."

"The other children?" Loki asked.

"No, not them," she said. "I was kept in this tiny, claustrophobic room, isolated except for meals and classes. Several women on the staff were always around. They bullied me and beat me. It was like they were constantly testing me—watching to see what I would do."

"Did no one show you kindness?" Gunnolf frowned.

"The ones who did weren't allowed to stick around long," she shrugged, "Either way, I learned to keep my distance."

"Which explains your fear of intimacy," Gunnolf nodded, eyeballing her like an exotic flower in a mountainside greenhouse.

"Hilarious," Loki snorted. "The man who refuses to meet with a therapist is now diagnosing others."

It was wisdom, not cowardice! Wren's temper spiked at his words. She flung a hand into the air in Gunnolf's direction. The water in the glass centerpiece vibrated with energy. The heavy crystal shattered, flower petals falling everywhere. Meanwhile, the water defied physics, forming a hand that flung the small rocks towards the man's arrogant face.

"I do not," she shouted, "have a fear of intimacy!"

A surprised Gunnolf threw up his palms. His wolf's quick instincts were the only thing that saved his face from a few broken teeth. The two-toned objects fell, thumping against the table, as he lowered his hands and raised his eyebrows at her.

She glared back at him, just as surprised at the incident and still offended he'd implied there was something wrong with her emotionally. There was also a little guilt about the table, but she got over that part pretty quickly. So what if she'd dented or scratched the damned thing? Some heavy-handed jackass had already split it straight down the middle.

"You protest too loudly," the heavy-handed jackass answered, adding a pointed, "mate."

"Okay," Loki speculated, looking from from one to the other, "so these people, or whomever they worked for, wanted access to her powers."

"My what?" she snapped at Gunnolf's younger brother, wondering at what point he'd lost his mind.

"Do you know many other people that can throw things without touching them, little birdie?" Loki asked, angling his head at the remnants of the centerpiece as he pointed to them.

"No," she admitted begrudgingly.

"How many?" Loki pressed her for the answer everyone seated at the table already knew.

None.

"This is ridiculous," Wren argued. She refused to speak the answer, folding her arms over her chest and slumping back against her chair. "That was not intentional— I don't have powers."

"Perhaps, mit hjerte," Gunnolf spoke gently, "there is more to you than meets the eye. Take a moment to consider what you have done. You say the action was not intentional, but it was your anger that caused it."

Wren gritted her teeth, stopping short of suggesting that maybe all that handsome arrogance deserved a chipped tooth or two to take it back down a notch. Words that spiteful were childish and embarrassing, and, if she were honest with herself, some part of her traitorous heart was saddened at the prospect of speaking them. It was better, all the way around, to keep her mouth shut.

"He is right," Loki chimed in, "and, agent of Odin or otherwise, someone out there wants to kill you. We are warriors. Help us to see the why and the how of this gift of yours, so we can teach you how to use it as a weapon."

Gunnolf shot a look of agreement in his brother's direction before shifting his gaze to Wren. He picked up a wet rock in his hand and asked her, "What were you thinking of before this happened?"

"I need to see Daisy," Wren said.

"You were contemplating Daisy just before trying to break my face?" Gunnolf raised his eyebrows in disbelief.

"No," she sighed, hating him for being such a smartass. "I was not."

"Forget her for now," Gunnolf said in a way that brooked no argument. "Your friend is not the one receiving death threats—if you want to speak with her, I will let you call her. And we will find people to handle any upcoming classes you have at the Nest while we explore your capabilities."

Loki agreed, "It is a wise idea. Sylvie has deep roots in the community here and also in the valley—I will enlist her help in following up on Daisy's lead."

"Fine," She reluctantly agreed, gazing at the small stone in Gunnolf's palm and wondering how much weirder her life was going to get. "In answer to your question, I had been thinking that I had a connection to the rocks, somehow, and wondering if I could feel them. Turns out I could—and, then, you pissed me off."

CHAPTER TWENTY-FIVE

"You manipulated water—this is not something naiad's can do. We need more of an explanation than it turns out you could, mit hjerte," Gunnolf prompted. He pushed the pebble in a circle, around the network of lines in his flattened palm, as he spoke.

"Stop calling me that," Wren snapped. "You're not sweet-talking me into procreation."

"Fine," he responded with a twist of his lips that clearly said he didn't believe her, "but you still need to explain, min skat."

Loki smothered a laugh with the knuckles of one hand and tried passing it off as a cough. When Wren demanded he translate what Gunnolf had said, he responded with my treasure.

"I'm not sure I can explain it," she shrugged. "Whether it's a trickle from the tap or the rushing of the lake during a storm, water has always soothed me. As a child, I connected to it more strongly than I did to people."

"Except for Florence," Gunnolf stated.

There was no question in his mind that had been the case. Or that the elf's selflessness had not been in vain— Florence had given his future mate a lifeline during a very dark time. If not for the love she provided, the woman sitting before him might have turned out differently.

"Yes," Wren agreed, "except for her. Florence was a

godsend."

"Literally," Loki interjected, picking up a sliver of the colorless crystal. He held it up, angling it until the overhead light shone through—the resulting prism of colors revealed a startling complexity. "Have you ever asked yourself why?"

"Because it was Freya's will to save the mother of my future children," Gunnolf answered authoritatively. He ignored whatever obscenity Wren muttered in response, more concerned that his brother was thinking too hard. An overly contemplative Loki was a Loki that was up to something—something that, undoubtedly, would lead them all into trouble.

"But there have been other descendants over the years. Lovely as Wren is, why her specifically?" Loki challenged, his blue eyes catching fire with a mischievous light. "The gods have been tricky since time began, brother. Freya is no exception. Open your ears and your eyes, if only for a moment, to think for yourself. Wren has a power that naiads do not. The naiad side always comes from a mother. We have no idea who her father is—so we still only have a partial tale."

Gunnolf glanced over at Wren, whose eyes were locked on Loki. Was she that interested in what his brother had to say or was it an interest in Loki himself? Damn him for being so light-hearted and charming.

"Nonsense," Gunnolf thundered a bit louder than intended, "Freya does not lie!"

"I don't think Loki is talking about a lie," Wren said, dipping her index finger into a drop of water lingering on the table as if it held the secrets of the cosmos, "at least not in the technical sense. Unless we're discussing moral theology."

"Which I would never do because it is a useless

pastime," Loki responded with a grin.

There it was, the willful godlessness, again—but there might be something to Loki's reasoning this time. Gunnolf set the stone down and rubbed at his forehead tiredly, feeling every last one of the centuries behind his age.

"So," he said. "You believe there has been a deliberate omission on Freya's part?"

"Yes," Loki answered, "and it is large one, involving both the little birdie's origins and the goddess's intentions."

"Hold on a minute. I thought your knocking me up was supposed to be all about satisfying the blood debt," Wren frowned at Gunnolf.

"And Freya outsmarting her husband," Loki added, "which all still holds true. You cannot fault Gunnolf. Odin's death wish was all we had proof of until you threw rocks without using your hands."

Gunnolf stared at his mate's lovely features—those soft pink lips, so pleasurable to kiss, and her wonderfully expressive eyes. She was vibrant and beautiful, the picture of youth and health—living proof of what Florence had traded to see to her happiness.

Mine, his wolf insisted.

It's not that easy, he responded, especially with Loki encouraging her rebellion. She is not likely to submit just because we sink our teeth into her neck and tell her to.

"I didn't throw them intentionally," she insisted. "One minute, I was thinking about rocks. The next, he pissed me off, and the damned things were in motion."

"Heading straight for my skull" Gunnolf stressed, still mildly insulted, "which is something I would never do to you."

"Oh, dear. Lady chivalry is dead," Loki said, twirling a finger in the air to indicate how little he cared.

Gunnolf gripped the table and growled, "Do not mock me, you little shit."

"Get over yourself, you big shit," his younger sibling replied, unperturbed. "There are far more important things to focus on, here, than you playing the big, powerful Alpha."

"Oh my god," Wren said, jumping up to stare at the two of them in blatant disbelief. "I am so glad I never had siblings. I swear, the two of you together are worse than Daisy's four-year-old."

"My therapist and I have talked about this kind of behavior, too," Loki suddenly told Gunnolf with a wink. "Height is a psychological advantage. The little birdie seeks to stand taller, towering over us to establish her dominance."

Wren blinked at him, clenched her jaw, and bellowed, "I am standing because I am tired of sitting across the table from two gigantic morons incapable of acting like spoiled children around one another."

"She will make an excellent mother," Gunnolf smiled, catching on to the game.

Wren's eyes lit up with fury, and she flicked her wrist. Sudsy dishes rose from the water Loki had left in the sink, flying across the room to break in two against the backs of Gunnolf and Loki's heads. Both brothers barked in pain and clutched at the growing knots beneath their hair.

"Well," Loki chuckled, "we are slowly and systematically destroying our kitchen, but, at least, there were no forks and knives involved."

"Agreed," Gunnolf said, turning his chair around and bending over to pick up pieces of their china, "and we know for certain that the key to accessing her powers, at least, for now, is emotion."

Wren glared at both of them, ruffling a hand through her bangs and responded, "I don't like being manipulated,"

"Neither does Gunnolf," Loki replied, "and Freya has been doing an excellent job of it up until now."

"Make no mistake," Gunnolf grumbled, placing the remains of shattered dinnerware on the cracked table, "whatever powers you hold, and whatever the goddess may have done to get her hands on them, you are still my mate. I will protect you."

"We'll see," Wren answered, noncommittally, before Loki began asking questions about anything else from her past that might hold a clue.

Gunnolf tried to listen attentively to her answers and even interjected a query, here and there. All the while his ecstatic, wolfy heart raced ahead into the future, drumming up idyllic visions of a lifetime of happiness with Wren.

We'll see. That was a far cry from no. Stubborn and proud as she was, this was a battle he could win.

CHAPTER TWENTY-SIX

"You honestly heard Freya talking to him?" the bare-chested Loki asked a ponytailed, barefoot Wren over the driving rhythm of "Master of Puppets"—a heavy metal compromise with which both brothers felt she could deal.

"Uh-huh," she answered, quickly leaning away and to the left as Gunnolf's brother dove for her right forearm.

She'd been hesitant about combat training, at first, but Gunnolf had insisted. Along with figuring out how to wield what Loki ridiculously dubbed her superhero power, they wanted her physically conditioned to fend off an unexpected attack. After a week and a half, she found that she enjoyed battling the men, and it was slowly restoring a feeling of control that had been missing from her life for far too long.

Loki's fingers missed her forearm, circling her wrist, instead. Her right leg lifted, chambering to execute a hard sidekick to his thigh before he could yank her body against him. Had he been a real attacker, she would have aimed a bit lower to break the kneecap.

"I think it pissed her off," she said.

"With good reason," Gunnolf grunted, grabbing Wren's shoulders from behind after Loki let go. He slapped a hand over her mouth and hooked the other across the front of her chest, dragging her into his warmth. "It is something only another god—one tied to me and listening very closely—should have heard."

"Then how did mmph?" was all she got out as the flat of his palm rudely sealed off the question. Her nostrils flared, inhaling the familiar scent that enveloped her—it was musky, entirely masculine, and divine.

Damn the man.

She widened her stance, softened her knees, and bit down, hard, on the meat between his forefinger and thumb. As he yelped and let go, she dropped down into sumo stance and grabbed the one hand still clutching her. Flipping her inside leg over behind his muscular thigh, she leaned forward and punched him in the adductor muscles, as close to his balls as she dared, before slipping away.

"Then how did I hear her?" It was amazing she even managed to get the question out.

"I have spoken with Sylvie," Loki countered, lunging for her while Gunnolf doubled over, instinctively cupping his testicles. "Why did you not tell us your real name was Ran?"

"What's my birth name got to do with...?"

Wren's sentence cut off when her knees hit the ground. Hard. She propelled her elbow upward into Loki's groin more roughly than intended in enthusiastic response to the stab of pain. Loki doubled over with a hiss of air, recovering enough to dive on top of her before she could scramble backward out of his reach.

Gunnolf growled low in his throat. It was an oddly sympathetic sound—it was also the only reason Loki got away with what he did next. Holding Wren's hands above her head, he stretched out on top of her, for a moment, the wolf glowing red in his eyes. The wall of his chest was flush against her, his weight threatening to crush her as he leaned down, scraping his fully extended fangs over a vulnerable spot on her neck.

"Hit a man where it hurts," Loki snarled in her ear, "and even the nicest of us turns nasty, little birdie—be prepared."

"I..." she squeaked, nodding her head. It was a rude reminder that the men with whom she was training were more than just men. Then again, she was supposed to be more than just a woman, wasn't she?

"I won't do it again," she said, clearing her throat. "Promise."

"That is enough training for today," Gunnolf responded, pulling his brother off her and reaching down to help her stand. His wandering fingers brushed the bare skin on her back, lingering as a stamp of possession.

"Easy, big brother," Loki laughed, picking up one of the towels near the door and dabbing the sweat from his face. "We have touched plenty of the same women quite comfortably and without incident in the past."

Gunnolf glared at his brother, exposing one of his fangs.

"But I will not encroach on what is clearly your territory," Loki added, "Since you seem to take this mating thing very seriously. Time to change the subject, anyway— we need to discuss the historical significance of names."

Wren moved to the far wall to retrieve her water bottle. She stared at the plastic container, not entirely happy with Loki's phrasing—he might as well have called her Gunnolf's property. The next time something like that happened in training, she'd try using the water inside of the plastic to slam the damned thing into the back of his head.

Not that she was above feeling a bit possessive, herself. She still felt fairly murderous at the thought of Gunnolf touching any other woman—casual flings shared with Loki were by no means exempt.

The ice inside of the cylindrical container rattled and clanked as she crossed the room. She sank down into a seated position on the padded floor and said, in response to Loki's change of topic, "If you mean my name birth name, Ran, Florence said it had something to do with mythology. Aside from that, we never got into it."

Loki and Gunnolf plopped down on either side of her, with their muscular legs extended, and explained. In Norse legends, Ran was the wife of Aegir. The two were giants that lived in splendor beneath the oceans and seas. They were said to be the very force that animated the waters, and they held great feasts to which they invited the gods.

"I was named for a giant and raised by a giant slayer?" Wren interrupted for a moment, ignoring the sharp looks she received for it. "No wonder the woman changed my name."

As it was with many couples, the brothers explained, there was a duality between husband and wife. Aegir was considered benevolent and gracious, an ever-attentive host, while Ran had a reputation for being a bit darker in actions and temperament. She wielded the power to raise storms and drown sailors. Together, Ran and Aegir had nine daughters, the goddesses of the waves, and it was through them that the power of the bloodline continued.

"So," Wren frowned, "you think my name is no coincidence—that I'm somehow tied to the bloodline of these gods, through Honoraria?"

"Yes," Gunnolf nodded, "and you must have the right genes for tapping into it. Even without knowing who your father is, it would explain much. Why those people pushed you in the orphanage, why Freya took such an interest in you, and why you could hear her talking to me."

"Even if that's all true, you were already on her side,"

Wren said. "Why not save herself the trouble and tell you?"

"Because of what I have been trying to make him see, all along," Loki answered. "The gods are tricky—Freya, especially. Berserker Wolves belong to Odin, and Freya wants power and dominion. You are the only reason Gunn would ever consider defying her husband. A powerful child, with the blood of Berserkers, Giants, and who knows what else in its veins, would make an excellent weapon for Freya. One that might tip the scales in her favor in a war against her husband."

"If she's so pissed off at Odin, why not just divorce him?" Wren asked.

"The gods do not believe in divorce," Gunnolf responded.

"But they believe in war," she said, dipping her head to pinch the bridge of her nose between thumb and forefinger. It wasn't enough pain to get rid of the panic that threatened to overwhelm her. "Okay, I'm going to be completely honest, here. I've had just about enough of everybody in the world making plans for my life without notifying me. So I'm going to take a nice, long shower and try and forget everything you just told me for a while."

CHAPTER TWENTY-SEVEN

Gunnolf eased his underwear down over his arousal, stepping out of them as they pooled on the cool tiles of the guest bathroom. The tiles in his bathroom had the luxury of a radiant heat system, but the space currently lacked something far more important. He fisted his aching cock, giving it a few lazy pumps as he watched Wren's naked body through the opaque shower door. The sexy yoga vixen looked delicious, squeezing all that liquid soap onto her pastel bath sponge.

He had tried as hard as he could to convince her to move into his room, but she just spouted more nonsense about prophylactics and autonomy. So he had purchased a year's worth of condoms, instead—they would only last a few months, considering how horny he was—and placed his stubborn little mate in the neighboring room.

"You need help," he announced, while stepping in behind her to grab her hips and pull her back against him.

"Hey! That's not a sponge rubbing against me," she countered, trying to hand him the mesh knit rubbing tool over one shoulder.

"Sponge administration is your job," he replied, holding her in place as he rocked his hips back and forth, sliding his sensitive erection up and down her back. He hunched to nibble at one shoulder, watching the water spray onto her pebbled nipples with a smile. "I am only here to help you rub and lather."

"You mean you're only here to molest me, you big pervert," she muttered, rubbing the sponge over the opposite shoulder, across her neck, and down to her chest.

"Would you like me to stop being perverted?" he asked, sliding his hands higher to intervene. He massaged her firm, orange blossom scented breasts, protecting them from the sponge.

"No," she moaned, arching her back to push her breasts deeper into his hands.

"Well, then," he growled into her ear, rolling her nipples between his fingertips. He teased them into hardened peaks. "You had better keep that sponge moving, woman."

She slid the sponge around in circles—rib-to-rib, hip-to-hip, and lower. A gasp echoed in the shower around them as the rough netting made contact with her clit.

"No," Gunnolf told her when she arched her hips toward the material, "not yet—have you forgotten the golden rule?"

"I haven't," she answered breathlessly, wiping the sponge in between her legs, once more, before moving on to her thighs.

"Tell me," he prompted. Although pleased his mate had stopped when he said no, the wolf inside of him needed to hear it. It was one of the few acts of submission she was willing to give.

"I can't cum without your permission, you bastard," she said.

"Bastard is preferable to yeti," he responded with a chuckle, letting his fingers drift over her backside. He smacked her ass playfully when she bent over. "Put more soap on the sponge and hand it to me. I will tend to your back while you shampoo your hair."

"I thought you said sponge administration was my job," she challenged, squeezing more liquid onto it from the plastic bottle with the flowers painted on its label.

"I did," he agreed, as she handed it to him and reached for the shampoo, "but I changed my mind. I cannot fuck you as thoroughly as I intend to, in the shower, min skal."

"You know you're going to smell like a girl, now," she told him.

He laughed, running the sponge over a shoulder blade jutting out at an angle. His mate's entire body—every hollow and curve, every muscle, sinew, and bone—was amazing.

The woman was a work of art made explicitly for his enjoyment.

"I will smell like my mate—as I should," he answered, pausing to sink playful teeth into her right buttock as he squatted down to attend to her calves and ankles.

"We will both smell like sex, again," she sighed. "I have had no idea why I even bother bathing, anymore."

"My sentiments exactly," he responded, climbing back to his feet. "I have no idea why you insist on wasting perfectly good nudity."

He hung the sponge up by its hook on the wall and helped rinse out her long, soft hair. All the while, he was thinking of how much he looked forward to the feel of it on his belly and thighs as her sweet mouth moaned around his cock. If she would only open her heart to him as willingly as she did her lips, things would be easier between them.

Bite her, the wolf said, reminding him that he did not need permission.

I will not risk her running away from us, he responded silently, stepping out onto the mat. He reached for a fluffy towel he had grabbed from the dryer not long ago. She is frightened enough of what she feels as it is.

We will lose her, the wolf whined.

We will not, Gunnolf assured it as Wren stepped out behind him and held out her arms, allowing him to envelop her body in warm, luxurious cotton. She likes our game of master and thrall too much. We must be patient, and her heart will follow.

CHAPTER TWENTY-EIGHT

Wren shivered at the feel of Gunnolf's large hands through the cotton. The towel smelled like the ocean—he must have figured out her favorite fabric softener. It was touching and deeply disconcerting that a man so domineering paid so much attention to the little things.

She glanced up into the blue eye staring down at her so intently. At times, it felt as if he were trying to peel back all her layers and peer into her soul. Why couldn't he just let it go? Sex with him was fine, more than fine, really, but it was hard to imagine ever being ready the other kind of vulnerability, again.

"I'm not sure I get you..." she mused, running a hand over his jaw and enjoying the rough familiarity of the stubble.

"There is no need to," he responded with a smile, nuzzling her hand with his cheek and chin as she took the towel with her other hand. "You cannot get what you already have."

"You're still wet," she sidestepped, grabbing a fresh towel from the nearby countertop.

Standing on tiptoe, she rubbed at his thickly corded muscles, starting with his arms and chest. The man was magnificent. He was a marble sculpture with a massive cock and a beautiful V-shaped cut to the muscles of his lower abdomen—an Adonis belt of which even Adonis should be jealous.

"So are you," he answered, sliding two fingers between her legs to tease her pussy before driving them inward to prove his point.

She inhaled sharply, dropping the towel, and he fucked her with his digits until she was panting and pleading. When she was riding on the edge of orgasm, he withdrew, tapping his fingers against her mouth so she could lick them clean.

When she had finished, he bent down, putting one arm behind her knees and the other at the back of her shoulders to sweep her off her feet. The two of them went, stark naked, down the hallway, with him carrying her like some blushing bride to his room, where he kicked the door shut behind them.

"I can't believe you did that," she said, falling onto the bed where he dropped her, with a small bounce and a shake of her damp hair. The man had some nerve. "What if Loki saw us?"

"Public exposure is the price you must pay for a separate room," Gunnolf shrugged, raising an eyebrow for a moment as he towered over her. "So what if he sees us—are you worried he might die of envy? You should not be thinking of my brother, or speaking his name, while lying naked on my bed."

"Fine," she responded, sitting up to capture the moisture seeping from the top of his bobbing cock with a flick of her tongue, "Loki who?"

Although he was flippant, she knew the possessiveness that drove his comments well enough and, at times, even felt a begrudging fondness for it. Wrapping her fingers around his thick shaft, she watched the pleasure flood his face at her grip. She tightened her hand just a fraction, pumping him slowly.

He had tormented her—turnabout was only fair.

Her flattened tongue swept over the crown of his dick before darting away to skirt and twirl around its sensitive underside and edges. Still stroking him a bit too gently for his tastes, she returned to lap at a new round of salty pre-cum in the center.

He twitched.

"You're not the only one whose body is a playground," she laughed, relishing the rough sound he made when she parted her lips around the velvety, musk-scented tip of his erection.

"That feels so good," he groaned, reaching down to fondle her breasts and tease her nipples while she sucked and stroked him, "but you will stop. I do not wish to cum yet."

"Who said I would let you cum?" she asked, raising an eyebrow to mock him.

"Try and stop me," he growled at her, flashing a playful fang as his hands tore open one of several colorful condom packets piled on the bedside table.

She grabbed a pillow to cushion her head, lying down and openly admiring his body as he rolled the material, tip first, over his mountainous cock. It was a non-negotiable part of the deal—one the arrogant man accepted with grace only after initially arguing until he was red in the face that latex was unnatural and, surely, her birth control pills would be enough.

It shouldn't be necessary, the voice inside of her nagged, not with our mate.

Here's an idea, she responded as he lay down alongside her, dipping his lips to her ear and stretching a hand across her belly. Why don't you shut up so we can enjoy the damned mating part?

"That pussy needs to be fucked, now, doesn't it?" he rumbled in her ear, capturing her wrists with one hand.

"Yes," she breathed, arching her hips as his fingers traced light circles against her sensitive skin. They trailed from her belly button down to her mons, barely brushing the bundle of nerves at the bottom.

"Yes, what?" He licked at her ear.

"Yes, fuck me," she groaned, her already aching pussy growing wetter.

"But," he nibbled at the delicate lobe, this time, rubbing his cock against the side of her leg, "you know that's not the right way to ask."

"Gunnolf, please," she moaned—the man was driving her insane.

"Please, what?" His expression was smug as he continued the torture. "And speak up, so I can hear you."

"Please," she raised her voice just a little, squirming beneath his fingertips. Loki was home, and his hearing was perfect—Gunnolf's game was obviously meant to drive the point of ownership home, "Please, Master—I need to feel you inside of me. Please fuck my pussy."

"That is very sweet," he answered, moving down between her legs in a flash. He gripped them spreading her wide, but stopped short, with the head of his cock positioned at her entrance. "Sweet words from a lovely mouth—but you know it is not enough. Tell me what you are and what you need."

"Master, please," she locked eyes with him.

"Who do this beautiful body belong to?" he coaxed. "There is no need for shame. Let go of it, mit hjerte. Give your master what he wants so he can give you what you need."

"It's yours, Master—I'm your fuck toy," she answered him, loudly, her face turning red. She felt the tip of his cock nudge her pussy for just a moment, taunting her.

"And who owns this wet, hungry little pussy?" he prompted.

"You do," she answered.

"Very good—and what should I do with my pussy? Hmm?" he said. "Even louder, this time, unless you wish to find out what it is like to be spanked, instead."

"Fuck your pussy," she answered, raising her voice. "Please, Master, use your fuck toy."

"With pleasure," the handsome bastard smiled, sliding his heavy cock into her.

CHAPTER TWENTY-NINE

"Gods, you are perfect," he said, pausing to rest his forehead against hers now that his cock was where it wanted to be.

"Am I?" she teased. "Because you're not—you're heavy, and those hips are not thrusting. Fucking me involves lots of thrusting."

"I should spank you for that," he answered, pushing himself up on his arms to relieve her of some of the pressure from his weight.

The truth was, his mouth watered at the thought of it. He could picture her, wriggling in his lap while that gorgeous little backside bounced and reddened beneath his palm. His dick swelled even more at the thought as he rocked his hips back and forth.

Her breathing hitched and quickly turned to panting for him.

"You can do it later," she moaned, shuddering at a sudden change in angle that applied more pressure to her sweet spot, "Please, don't stop."

He dipped his head for a sweet kiss, and she closed her eyes, avoiding his gaze. He captured her lips more roughly than intended in response, turning the kiss into a bruising thing. She was his mate. He deserved all of her, damn it—not just her body.

"There is no sense in being afraid, you know," he

frowned, pushing his torso up, again, and increasing the tempo.

"I'm not afraid," she muttered, her eyes still closed. Her brows furrowed in concentration, her hips rising to meet his thrusts and match the pace.

"Then, why will you not look at me?" he demanded, slamming into her and enjoying the way that she clenched around him.

"Why do you have to control everything?" she panted, gripping the bed and arching even more.

"That is not an answer,"Gunnolf responded, vowing to break through her stubborn defenses one way or another.

He knew exactly how close she had been to release when he withdrew abruptly, flipping her sweat-slick body over and positioning her on her hands and knees on the mattress.

"You are such an asshole," she ground out through her teeth.

He gave her firm little bottom several hard smacks with the palm of his hand. The cracking sound still echoed in the room as he opened her legs wider, staring at the wet, swollen lips of her pussy, and the tiny hole above them.

Mine, his wolf said.

He plunged the thumb of his right hand between her nether lips to gather moisture, while bending over her and stretching a finger up to strum lightly at her clit for a moment.

"In this room, I am not the lover and mate you take for granted," he corrected her in a velvety voice. Smacking her ass cheeks, he swirled his thumb in circles inside of her. "I am supposed to be your master—something we will make sure you cannot forget, min skat."

He stopped when he heard the first sobs, knowing

Wren was in discomfort, yet still incredibly turned on, from the volley of slaps. Her pussy had grown even wetter while she dipped her head to the bed and arched her buttocks higher for him. Even now, she would let him continue, which was more than enough submission for his wolf—they had no intention of ever truly hurting her.

"And what a lucky master I am," he rumbled, pressing gentle lips to a soft patch of reddened skin. His thumb was still inside of her, his finger feathering over her clit, "I have such a pretty little fuck toy at my command and her pussy drips honey just for me."

She made a guttural sound, deep in her throat, her ass circling clockwise, her pussy now desperately following the motion of his thumb.

"You enjoy being used by your master," he observed, while his mate shamelessly churned her hips, begging and moaning for him like an animal in heat. "Don't you? You need this, hmm? You want to be owned and fucked by your mate, now, don't you?"

She whimpered, beyond words, and her movements became frantic.

"Answer me," he demanded.

"Yes," she managed to rasp for him.

"Then keep that beautiful ass in the air," he ordered, sliding his thumb from her pussy.

He positioned himself against the back of her thighs, stroking one hand gently up and down her lower back as he moved his opposite thumb, still slick with her pussy juices, up to circle her tiny puckered rosebud. He smiled when he she stiffened—this was definitely something new for her.

It was virgin territory for him to plunder.

"You will relax," he growled—at both her and his wolf, which was equally excited they were going be the first, there—as he slid his cock into her pussy.

His thumb stilled its circling while the opposite hand moving from the muscles of her back around to her clit. Rubbing at the bundle of nerves, he pumped his dick in and out of her.

She panted and rocked against him, fucking him back as he pressed the digit against the small, tight ring of muscle.

"Now," he said, "push out for me."

Surprisingly enough, she complied without argument. The tip of his thumb pushed in past the barrier. It was a snug fit, but she continued to open for him, allowing him in up to the first knuckle. All the while, she shuddered, her movements growing more frantic once the digit made it all the way inside.

He had her where he wanted—beyond words, enveloped and overwhelmed by the scent, smell, and feel of him. Nothing existed for Wren, now, but her lover and mate, and the pleasure he was giving her.

Now, his wolf demanded.

Gunnolf felt his fangs fully extend. He lost control the moment the first spasms ripped through her, milking his cock. Removing his thumb, he flipped her hair to one side and gripped her shoulders in a blur of movement. His teeth sank into the tender skin where her neck and left shoulder met, his mouth filling up with her magic and blood.

It was the most wonderful thing he had ever tasted.

As he came again, her scream of pain tearing through him, his mouth moved, snarling two words against her skin.

Forgive me.

CHAPTER THIRTY

"No more canceled meetings—I'm talking to Daisy in person, not calling her," Wren said flatly, refusing to look at the hulking figure lounging on the grass at her side.

The one call she'd been allowed to make had achieved nothing aside from negating their lunch date and gathering details on the contact from the orphanage for Loki and Sylvie to investigate. Gunnolf had sat there, listening, the whole time—an oppressive reminder that she was his mandatory houseguest. Not even a houseguest, an inmate on lockdown just as she had been in her early childhood. The only differences were an ugly wound and senses acutely attuned to the warden.

"And I'm going back to work, too," she added.

"No," Gunnolf answered, toying with her hair.

"No to what?" she demanded.

"No to both," he said.

Rather than wasting energy on replying or batting away a hand that would only return, Wren extended her hands out toward the lake and moved them in a stirring motion, coaxing a nearby patch of water into mirroring the chaos in her head. The section of the lake she had chosen churned, the same way her head had after Florence's death.

It was worse, now, knowing why the woman's body had failed. If not for Freya's stupid bargain, the former immortal would still be immortal—and alive. Instead, she had passed away in a cold hospital bed, blanketed by fear and the pungent scent of antiseptic from the hallway outside.

Be reasonable, the naiad pleaded, not all love leads to loss—he is immortal.

He deliberately hurt us, Wren answered.

You are too stubborn for your own good, the voice said.

Fuck you, Wren replied.

"There is no sense in fearing for your friend, if that is what you are thinking," Gunnolf spoke, interrupting her internal conversation. "Daisy is in no real danger. You, on the other hand, are. You need more training and a handle on fully accessing and controlling your powers before you can protect yourself."

"Don't you mean protect myself from everyone but you?" she asked, summoning a small wave to dampen his leather shoes.

"Those are foolish words you do not mean, min skat," he replied, adding in response to the look that she shot him, "I will not tell you I am sorry for biting you—for causing you pain, yes, but not for the bite."

"Of course, you're not," she spit the words back at him, jumping to her feet. The bite was a mark of ownership more permanent than any ring—one man shamed her by running, the other, now, by claiming her. "It's a giant neon billboard to your precious Freya and the rest of the world that I'm your property as much as Honoraria was Halvdan's!"

"My mark is not a stamp of slavery," he growled. "It has nothing to do with the games we play, you foolish, stubborn woman—it embodies my love and protection. Can you not see that you are far more precious to me than the gods or anything else on this earth?"

She stared up at a cornflower blue sky in exasperation—a patch of fluffy white clouds in a dragon formation wander by above then. Berserker Wolves, Elves, and the stinking magic in her veins all existed. Who was to say that dragons weren't real, too? They were probably more real than this delusional, fate-mandated love at first sight crap.

"You just met me," she dismissed the idea, with her head still pointed skyward. "A man can't love what he doesn't know."

"I know you as I know my own heart," he argued, trailing his fingers gently along her cheek. "You are my destiny."

"Based on what?" she laughed, bitterly. "The lies and machinations of a self-interested goddess desperate for us to fuck and make a super baby."

"You do not believe you are worthy of love," he stated.

"I do not believe in fairytales with happy endings," she glared at him, ignoring the ring of truth in his words. "I'm a Brothers Grimm kind of girl."

"But every once in a while..." he argued, shaking his head.

"Not with my story," she cut him off, knowing what he intended to say. "My tale doesn't magically get to end well, just because some sex-hungry Alpha control freak tries to force things in a direction they were not meant to go."

"There is nothing to force," he answered. "This was meant to be, and I am here, already—by your side, willing to give you everything."

"Once I've sacrificed all that I am," she countered. "You want me to give up my body, my business, and, probably, my only decent friend—you would have me surrender the sum of my existence in trade for you."

"What if I did?" he challenged angrily. "Have you had such a happy life that you would really lose something in trade?"

She ignored him, storm clouds gathering above the lake as her mind revised her story once again.

Once upon a time, there was a lovely maiden far away from home. She was lost, and tired, and wandering aimlessly atop a great mountain when she stumbled upon a giant wolf at rest in a clearing. He bit her—hurt her—and yet, she still longed for him. Knowing that the creature was dangerous, that loving him could forever change her, she came to her senses and ran away. The End.

No, her argumentative naiad-half corrected, the lovely, brain-dead maiden did a stupid thing and ended up dying alone and miserable. It was the exact opposite of what the woman who adopted the maiden in the first place, sacrificing her immortality, would have wanted for her.

"I can't do this with you anymore," Wren said, more to herself than anyone else, as she twisted and jumped to her feet.

The dragon clouds veered back toward the lake, erupting into a storm above the water. A flash of lightning crackled overhead. The sound chased her troubled heart, all the way back to the lake house, through the trees.

CHAPTER THIRTY-ONE

"No matter what you may think of me, you are still in danger. I would never forgive myself if anything happened to you," Gunnolf said, uncrossing his arms to stroke her hair.

He couldn't help himself—even his wolf felt the need to comfort her.

The woman from the orphanage appeared to have vanished, and it wasn't surprising considering what rumors Loki and Sylvie had managed to dig up about the place so far. Despite its bare bones appearance, the institution once had serious backing—some variety of military money—and it was said to have been uniquely interested in children with latent magic in their genes. The odds were good that they had allowed Wren's adoption only after their efforts had failed, wanting to see if a different environment would trigger her powers.

Of course, Gunnolf realized, the odds were also good that his mate would never forgive him for holding her captive.

Since her outburst a few days ago, Wren had become silent and withdrawn. Her eyes remained downcast. She would barely eat or communicate, and even the news about the orphanage's supposed military roots hardly fazed her. While she still endured combat training, her performance was purely mechanical. There had been no more attempts from her to test or strengthen the connection between the emotions she had shut off and the water, either.

Even in bed—because, gods help him, he still couldn't stop himself from needing her there—her responses were muted and sad. He had never imagined the feisty little woman capable of acting this way, but a nagging instinct told him what he was witnessing. This was a learned behavior—a deliberate act of self-preservation, once practiced by a child who had abandoned all hope in an orphanage. All her joy was gone because something had threatened it.

Not something, his wolf told him. It was us—we did this to her.

"I would never forgive myself if something happened," he clarified when she didn't respond to his touch, "but I also realize how wrong it is of me, being so inflexible This situation cannot be ideal—stuck here, day in and day out, missing your daily routine and your friends."

"Daisy," Wren said, looking up at him. "Her name is Daisy."

"Daisy," Gunnolf nodded, pleased to at least warrant eye contact from her again. "I have discussed your returning to work with Loki and Sylvie. They have agreed that, so long as one of us is available to accompany you, you may go. The same applies to meeting with Daisy."

"There are things I would like to say to her without a jailer present," she insisted.

No, the wolf snarled, Daisy will take her away from us.

He couldn't help but agree with his wolf that, in her current mindset, escape was most likely to be the topic of conversation.

"Nonsense," he answered. "At this point, secrets can only jeopardize your safety. Any conversations you have will be in front of one of us or not at all."

"Okay, Hitler," she said flatly, picking up a forkful of scrambled eggs with a dash of hot sauce on them, "but you left out something important. When do I get to return home?"

"You are home," he answered, watching her go from peacefully chewing a mouthful of breakfast to mouthing shards of broken glass in response to his words.

"No," she answered, putting down the fork to reach for a warm coffee cup with the Fenric Fitness logo painted on it. "This is not my home. I am being detained, in the finest prison in all of Elation, by a twisted bastard who has branded me with his teeth and regards me as a possession."

"You are behaving like a child," he said.

"You are treating me like one," she answered.

He fought the urge to growl and promised himself some time venting his frustrations on a punching bag, later. Maintaining the appearance of civility and kindness were crucial. The conversation was not heading in the direction he had intended, but, for the moment, she had resumed talking to him in complete sentences. It was a sign of progress between them, however small.

"Loki will take you to work today," he announced, pulling her cell phone from his pocket. The way she raised her eyebrows at the gesture did not go unnoticed, but he wisely kept his mouth shut about that, too. "Stay for a few hours and meet with the people I am paying to handle your classes. Call Daisy to come and visit you, there, if you wish. Or you may arrange for her to meet you and Loki for lunch somewhere close to the gym."

She ran her finger in circles along the rim of her coffee

mug, clenching her jaw for a moment before asking him, "Would you like to coordinate the timing of my bowel movements, as well, or am I still allowed to do that without your express permission?"

"I have asked that question, myself, more than once over the centuries" Loki chuckled, wandering in just in time to catch the tail end of their conversation.

Gunnolf looked over into Loki's twinkling eyes. His brother, too, was relieved to see a bit of Wren's will to fight returning. It made him mindful of a saying of which their mother had once been fond: It is the still and silent sea, not the turbulent one that drowns a man.

"He asks, and I answer that I prefer anything and everything pertaining to his ass remains a mystery to me," Gunnolf grumbled, taking a closer look at his brother's outfit. "What in the hell have you got on your feet, man—do you seriously intend to guard my mate wearing sandals?"

"These are rugged all-terrain sandals," Loki defended his choice of apparel with a wink at Wren. "I figured women who were into yoga would find them appealing."

"Trust me, Loki," Wren laughed, her face lighting up for a moment, "you don't need them. None of them will be looking at your feet."

"Enough chatter," Gunnolf growled. What had Loki done to deserve the woman's smile? "Go upstairs and get dressed before I change my mind about letting you go."

CHAPTER THIRTY-TWO

"So, yeah," Daisy said, her brown eyes glued to the mountain of muscle and charisma Wren had introduced to her as Loki, "how's it going?"

"My life is a giant shit-show. I'm being held prisoner as a sex slave in whatever the Viking version of a gulag is, and there's a freaking bite mark on my shoulder," Wren answered testily. She set the floral-patterned porcelain teapot down on the table and snapped her fingers twice. "Hey! I'm over here, married lady."

Sure, the frustration in her voice held more than just a tinge of anger, but she didn't care. Women had been talking to her while looking at Loki Fenric all morning. She expected the behavior from clients, but Daisy? Really?

"It is not that bad," Loki, who was far more comfortable than Wren had hoped he would be amidst the lavender and lace of The Tea House, assured Daisy with a wink, "although my brother is enough to drive any sane person crazy."

"I know this woman all too well—it's a short drive," Daisy answered dryly, flinching as a foot met her shin under the table. She turned to Wren and said, "Don't you kick me! I'm married, not dead. That is Grade A man candy over there—and a sex slave, honey? If his brother looks anything like this, I have no idea why in the hell are you even complaining about it. So he gave you a hickey—big deal."

Wren paused, picking at the food on her plate as a slender nineteen-year-old with perky boobs, blonde highlights, and odd violet contacts in her eyes interrupted, for the third time. She asked if they needed anything from her, anything at all. Wren slapped a palm down on the table and aggressively cleared her throat. The woman shot an odd look at her as Loki shook his head and thanked her, politely, for the attentiveness before sending her on her way. After that, thankfully, the girl hovered over the other tables around them but did not return to theirs.

The sandwich on Wren's plate was one of her favorites. Sadly, even artichoke with red pepper, sun-dried tomato, and goat cheese couldn't improve her temperament. She had desperately wanted to see Daisy, without a stinking babysitter, to discuss how conflicted she was, but her privacy and preferences no longer mattered. Hell, she could probably count herself lucky that Loki allowed her a meatless lunch, considering Gunnolf's concerns about her diet.

"Oh, I don't know," Wren responded, raising her voice as she lifted the bread from the top of her meal. She removed all the tomatoes—the damned things were supposed to have iron in them. "I'm probably just complaining because I've been kidnapped and held hostage by a delusional, controlling jerk who mistook my shoulder for rump roast and is determined to pump me full of his super sperm!"

Daisy raised her eyebrows, looking at the shocked faces around them and then at Loki, who continued being far too comfortable in a room full of nothing but busybodies and china patterns.

"It is not my sperm she is talking about," he shrugged, leaning back in his chair after taking another sip of tea.

"Wren," Daisy suggested quietly, "if you ever want to eat here again, you ought to lower your..."

"Oh, and, aside from this, which you refuse to take seriously," Wren interrupted, sliding the collar of her shirt down over one shoulder to give Daisy a glimpse of what was fast becoming a permanent scar from Gunnolf's fangs. "Do you want to know what the best part is? Somebody spray-painted a death threat all over my mailbox at home."

"Jesus" Daisy responded, already wide-eyed from seeing the hickey on steroids. "What did it say?"

"Die, bitch," Wren answered.

"Oh, my God." Daisy raised a spotless manicure, with the little white and yellow flowers for which she'd been named, to her lips. "This is because I found that woman for you, isn't it?"

"Probably," Loki mumbled around a mouthful of food. He set down the remnants of his third sandwich, hastily swallowing the part he'd been chewing. "That is why Gunnolf and I agreed it was best that we keep her with us, where we can protect her."

"Where they can maul me," Wren countered.

"They?" Loki retorted, teasing her. "You and Gunn never invite me to join the party. Not once have I been asked to spank that lovely ass or make you pant and moan—and Gunn will not let me be a handler for your battery-operated boyfriend. What do you call him, again, little birdie—Mongo?"

The sound of shattered china followed by a senior citizen's startled apology for splattering tea all over the others at her table came from nearby. One of her companions spoke up for the rest of them, fanning her flushed face with a napkin and responding that it was completely understandable.

"You're incorrigible, just like your brother," Wren sighed, still despondent. She had been wolf-napped, and her best friend was more preoccupied with the volume at which they discussed it. "I knew I should have asked for Sylvie today."

"Really?" Loki gave her a sideways glance before responding, "That is very open-minded of you. I was sure you would not want sexy Sylvie around—you know, since she was naked in Gunnolf's room, drinking scotch with him, right after he met you."

"She was what?" Wren felt guilty for shouting, although it was kind of her thing, because she had just decided to try and regulate her voice for Daze.

That woman loved all the frump and circumstance at the Tea House.

"Oops," Loki answered, fighting off a self-satisfied grin. "My apologies, I thought he told you. If it is any consolation, the event did not seem to be a big deal. As a matter of fact, Sylvie came to my room, afterward, to join the marathon sex with the other girls from the party—so, there is probably nothing to worry about."

Whether Loki had been trying to make her jealous or simply rendering a verbal slap to yank her out of the doldrums, it worked. She now knew Gunnolf slept with another woman on the same night he met her. Was everything the asshole said, all that destined mate, you are mine talk, bullshit? Maybe he had been trying to knock up Sylvie—all the other women from the orgy, too. God, if so, he was no better than Steven!

Wren muttered about what an idiot she was and strove to get a handle on her temper. She knew, for a fact, that she had failed miserably once the tea in the pots and cups all around them began bubbling and boiling, causing a stir among the other patrons.

"What the...?" Daisy asked, her voice trailing away as she looked at all the tables around them.

"That would be Wren's doing," Loki offered, helpfully. "Because she cares about my control freak of a brother more than she is willing to admit."

"But how is she doing it?" Daisy responded, looking over at Wren as the liquid on the tables settled down. "Wren, I'm your best friend—why didn't you tell me you have super powers?"

"Because they're not that super—and I didn't know until recently," Wren answered quietly. She scooted closer, suddenly inspired, and made a huge production out of patting her friend's hand. It worked, distracting the two of them long enough for her to swipe the woman's car keys from the jacket on the back of her chair with the opposite arm.

"Well, missy, you've got some explaining to do," Daisy said.

"I'll explain soon," she promised, lowering her voice to add, "right now I need to use the bathroom—and I might be in there for a bit."

Technically, that wasn't a lie. Wren just omitted she was using the restroom to emancipate herself. The window in the Ladies Room made a perfect escape route and borrowing Daisy's sedan from the parking lot was just what she needed to get her life back under control. Once she reached the mobile home park, she was going to load a suitcase, jump in her car, and hit the road.

That's running, the naiad said. *Florence wouldn't approve.*

No, it's not, she answered. *It's an impromptu road*

trip, which is an entirely different thing.

CHAPTER THIRTY-THREE

"You are sure the information is legitimate?" Gunnolf asked, a deep furrow forming in his brow as he considered the tattered manila folder.

"Yes," Sylvie answered grimly, taking a seat across from him in an office chair, "though I'd feel better if I wasn't. This is some barbaric shit. My friend John's a good man, more importantly, a reliable one. A guy who uses file folders until they disintegrate because it's better for the environment isn't going to lie for a paycheck."

He nodded and opened up the file, still grateful Sylvie had pulled some strings for them. John was an old lover turned friend—one of many, undoubtedly. He was also a Private Investigator who had been capable of digging into the past of a now defunct orphanage. What he found, via one of his leads, was concrete proof of an old, hush-hush research effort titled Project Elemental that had been funded by the Department of Defense.

The evidence wasn't pretty—faded pictures telling a tale of torture, genetic enhancements, and experimentation. One, in particular, caught Gunnolf's eye. It was a black and white image of a naked woman, with a bruised face and haunted eyes, standing next to an expressionless man in a lab coat and wire-rimmed glasses. The adult female looked so much like Wren that it made him want to kill someone.

The phrase viable subject was scrawled, in faded ink,

on the back of the photo.

"Viable for what?" he asked, hoping, against all the odds, that the answer wasn't something horrifying. After a lifetime of thinking herself abandoned, the news would break Wren's heart all over again.

"You know what," Sylvie said, her lips twisting with distaste. "Forced breeding, with someone or something. Wren's birth mother couldn't have placed her in that orphanage. She was either dead or confined to a cage, somewhere, producing more offspring for them."

It was the same thing Freya—and he—had asked Wren to do.

Our home is not a cage, his wolf insisted, and we love her.

"Whoever was in charge of this nightmare deserves to die," he ignored its comment, flipping through the images.

There was a photo of several giant water tanks. A blurred, hulking figure was locked away in each of them. Larger than him in shifted form, these were probably beings that had never known kindness, let alone how to show it to a female smaller and weaker than them.

"Well," Sylvie responded flatly, looking down at the picture with him. "If you want my opinion, death is too good for these jerks. I asked John what those things are and where they came from, but he didn't have the answers. It seems like no one does. The only thing we know for sure is that you can name some variety of elemental being, just about anything you can imagine, and bet the humans running this thing captured one a test subject. They tried everything—from splicing genes and encouraging mutations to forced breeding."

Gunnolf remained silent, for a moment, still processing the information. His mate existed because of a twisted endeavor. Project Elemental had been in the business of warping the Supernatural to create human-made monsters with who knew what kind of capabilities How much Freya had known about this sordid business? Were there people out there still looking for Wren?

He looked over at Sylvie and asked, "Do we know if this horror show is still going on?"

"If so," Sylvie shrugged, "it's found new funding. The Department of Defense pulled the plug. They washed their hands of it. John's not sure the DOD set the fire, though. It could just as easily have been Daisy's lead, the woman that recently disappeared. Or an angry child discovering his or her powers."

"Something worth looking into," he nodded. "There might be others still alive that we can help. I need you to be honest with me—did Florence ever do or say anything that might have indicated she knew what was going on?"

"No," she responded, shaking her head. "Trust me— the woman had no idea."

"She went to the orphanage to adopt Wren. Are you one hundred percent sure—no doubt whatsoever in your mind about it?" Gunnolf asked, watching closely to gauge her reaction..

"Positive," Sylvie snapped, her amber eyes glowing at the insult. "If Florence knew about this research shit, human or not, she'd have gathered forces to go in there and rescue those kids before burning the place to the ground. And I'd have been the one leading the rescue and lighting the match."

Satisfied with her answer, he went back to the pictures again. Toward the back, he noticed a few color photos taken more recently—pictures of Wren's trailer and the lot next door. There were two shots of the neighbor Loki had spoken with when he and Sylvie went to collect her things. Gunnolf recognized the man from his brother's description—wiry and unpleasant, with eyes that were hard to read.

Apparently, John must have thought so, too.

One of the snapshots featured him with the noisy white dog. The second picture was also in the yard only, this time, he was talking to a young blonde with odd violet eyes. She looked familiar, and she was young, too young and cute to be a creep's girlfriend, but there was no family resemblance between them.

"Your friend took photos of the neighbor," he said, tapping the image of the couple. "This woman, I think I have seen her hanging around outside the gym before. Does John know who this is?"

"Just somebody suspicious enough to warrant watching," Sylvie answered, flipping the photo over to the back to point out two question marks penned in black ink. "He thinks the eyes are for real. She might be the result of more recent experiments. If that's the case and she's in cahoots with the neighbor, well, they say when nasty things happen to someone, statistically, the most likely suspects are usually the people closest to them."

"And it does not get much closer than the man next door," Gunnolf finished the thought for her.

The more closely he looked at the two of them, the more his instincts told him they were dangerous. A mysterious woman with violet eyes and a creep with a poker face—they were the most likely source of the death threat. These two had been keeping an eye on his mate and plotting against her.

"What do you want to do about it?" Sylvie asked.

"Hit the road and warn Loki," he said. "He needs to

bring her home."

The shifter's expression changed noticeably with the mention of his brother's name. As far as Gunnolf was concerned, whether she had simply grown lonely without Florence or genuinely loved Loki, the two of them settling down together would not be a bad thing. Sylvie had ties to Wren because of Florence and a decent head on her shoulders. It was much more sensible than Loki's, whose heart was too damned fickle.

"I'll call," Sylvie offered just as he had anticipated she would.

"My brother has already met the man," Gunnolf nodded. "Make sure you describe the girl in detail."

CHAPTER THIRTY-FOUR

"Made it," Wren sighed.

She pulled Daisy's car—a new four-door sedan with the telltale scents of sugary cereal and children's toys in the back seats—on the grass beside her jalopy. On the bright side, with no one driving the old, beat up thing resting in the driveway, the crack in her back windshield hadn't spread any further. Of course, that would probably change when she drove down the mountain in search of a cheap hotel somewhere.

The dog next door popped its head up and ran over, barking and baying its greetings as she climbed out of the driver seat. For once, the awful ruckus was a welcome sound. It interrupted the strange question that popped into her head about whether or not she might, someday, come to terms with the idea of motherhood.

After all, Daisy had.

"Believe it or not," Wren said, kicking the thought aside as she walked a few steps in the howler's direction, "I missed you, you little jerk. But I'd miss you more if you didn't bark like a hell-spawned demon doggie at all hours of the day and night."

The neighbor's pickup truck sat next door, which probably meant Bud was home. He didn't come out to say anything. That was perfectly fine—he had always been creepy, and she didn't feel like speaking to him, anyhow.

Daisy's spare trailer key—the one she'd given her friend in case of emergencies—turned out to be less worn than her own. It worked like a charm, with a minimal amount of cursing and fumbling.

After so much time in the lake house, the mobile home felt even dinkier. Smallness aside, though, it was still hers, and, no matter how hard he tried, she would not give Gunnolf Fenric the satisfaction of keeping her away from it.

She removed her shoes and tossed the pile of junk mail retrieved from her poorly repainted mailbox onto the coffee table. Crossing a living room carefully decorated with accents and knickknacks from happier days, she told herself there was no point in hoping Loki had bothered to look in the refrigerator, let alone thrown anything out when he swung by to pick up Mongo and her things.

The white door opened with a faint click and the hiss of a stubborn seal giving way. Wilted salad, spoiled milk, and a few other things no one in their right mind wanted to smell all came wafting out in a rush of chilly air. The thought of throwing food away made her cringe. Wastefulness might not be a big deal to party boys with a lodge by the lake, but, for a woman used to living on a tight budget, it seemed inexcusable. Unfortunately, no one had swung by her cart at the grocery store to say hey, you might want to ease up on the perishable items because it's the day before your kidnapping.

After digging under the kitchen sink for a garbage bag, she held her breath, tossing the offending items into the thin plastic and trying not to think too hard about Loki's comments. So what if Gunnolf had sex with another woman? Wren was running away and didn't want to have his baby, anyhow.

Sylvie's not just any woman, the naiad reminded her.

She is beautiful and confident, with a body like a brick shit house.

Yeah, Wren answered. Thanks for the FYI, Rick James—but I don't care.

Oh, yes, you do, the naiad assured her.

She found a home for the stinky trash bag outside, by the front steps, and shifted gears to think about filling her suitcase and a box or two in the hall closet. It wouldn't take her lunch partners long to realize she wasn't coming back to the table. Daisy knew Wren well—the absence of her keys and sedan would be all the evidence the woman needed to put the pieces together.

In the meantime, Wren would pack the rest of her clothes, along with some pictures and a few mementos. Maybe she'd make room for a book or two. Anything other than philosophy—she'd burned out on Plato from reading through Gunnolf's bookshelves. Science fiction sounded appealing. There were all of her romance novels, too—no, now that she thought about it, those were staying put. As much as she loved the damned things, they encouraged optimism. She had to maintain a healthy sense of terror at the prospect of losing herself completely in Gunnolf's shadow—there was nothing sexy about being under house arrest for the rest of her life.

Hypocrite. Her inner voice was insistent as she folded the rest of her clothes and placed them in the suitcase. You know it isn't a prison. Home is where your heart and your mate are.

"Mate, kidnapper. To-may-to, to-mah-to," Wren muttered, pulling the rest of her clothes from the closet. "And you need to shut your pie-hole—all this barging into the head party where you were clearly not invited is annoying."

"Well, this is cozy," a feminine voice announced from the hallway behind her. "You and the friend in your head having a little chat, are you? I bet it's nicer than mine is to me."

Wren spun around, a black picture frame slipping from her grasp. One edge struck the floor, splitting its cheap plastic and cracking the glass. It was her favorite photo of Florence. She would have been even more upset about it, but the sight of the girl from The Tea House pointing a stubby, silver-barreled gun at her head told her she'd be better off rearranging her list of priorities.

"Who are you?" she demanded.

Hopefully, the answer wasn't coming with a bullet.

"I'm the bitch next door," the blonde said nodding in the direction of the trailer where the creepy neighbor lived. "The one who left a message for you."

"You live with Bud?" Wren thought of the words that had been on her mailbox, her heart hammering in her chest. "I've never seen you there."

"Yes, you have. You see me all the time," the girl replied, shifting the tip of her nose into a snout to prove it. "I dig up seashells and bark for you. Sometimes you've even talked to me—you just didn't know it until now."

CHAPTER THIRTY-FIVE

"I should have never let her leave the house," Gunnolf growled, fastening his seatbelt. "Put my brother on speaker. Now."

Though his hearing was good enough to pick up that the mysterious violet-eyed girl had been waiting tables at the restaurant, he was tired of not being in charge of the damned conversation. Plus, he was too furious at losing control of what should have been a simple situation to feign politeness after he and Sylvie climbed into his vehicle outside the gym.

Sylvie nodded, keeping her mouth shut. She lay her phone down in the center console, pushing a button to share the conversation and bumping up the volume while he turned his key in the ignition.

"Gunn," Loki said, the sound of a car horn nearby making it apparent that he was also pulling onto the road. "We are on our way."

"We?" Gunnolf asked.

"Yes, we," his brother replied. "I explained it might be dangerous, but Daisy insisted on coming."

"You're damn right I did." Daisy's voice came from somewhere in the background.

"Bro, will you at least let me explain?" Loki asked.

"Explain what?" Gunnolf barked. "That you have failed due to your incompetence? One of the people threatening my mate's life was right there, within arms reach, Loki. Now, both she and Wren are gone."

"Wren took Daisy's keys and her car. She wanted to go home, and that's where she went," Loki insisted. "What was I supposed to do, bro, follow her all the way into the women's bathroom like some pervert?

"You are a pervert," Gunnolf shouted, "and if potty detail is what it took to ensure her safety then, yes! You should have gone in there, parked your ass against the stall, and asked if she needed more toilet paper. That girl heard Wren complaining about how much she wanted to go home, too, and she knows exactly where that home is."

Gunnolf heard Daisy's voice saying things like see what she's saying and needs to back the fuck off in the background.

"I will be there, soon." Loki tried to assure him. "You and I will handle it. Panic helps nothing at this point. Besides, Daisy is right. Your mate is strong-willed and independent—and you are a domineering asshole, Gunn."

"I am an Alpha, not an asshole," Gunnolf argued, clenching his jaw and tightening his fingers around the steering wheel.

"Alpha, asshole, whatever—that is what I am trying to tell you. It is all the same thing to Wren," Loki answered, braking for a red light. "You and your wolf need to back off or risk losing the woman you love for good. Couple's therapy wouldn't be a bad idea, either."

"I will not sit back and allow my mate to take foolish actions that put her in danger—and quit throwing Glenda in my face like a self-help grenade," Gunnolf told him.

"But you need to understand: People do stupid things when they feel backed into an emotional corner," Loki responded. "You excel at taking charge and backing people into those corners, Gunn."

"You are sleeping with your therapist, aren't you?" Gunnolf retorted, knowing there would be no denial from his brother—then, he paused.

For once, he paused to consider the merit of Loki's words rather than dismissing them. The last thing he wanted to do was chase his mate away.

There was a rustling, and a click soon followed, after Daisy asked Loki to put his phone on speaker so she could talk to Gunnolf, directly.

"Umm, yeah," a feminine voice addressed him. "It's Gunnolf, right?"

"Yes," he answered.

"Wren said you wanted to do the whole family thing with her—settling down, making babies and whatnot. Is that right?" Daisy asked.

"Yes," Gunnolf responded, casting a glance in Sylvie's direction. "Why?"

Sylvie mouthed the words I have no idea.

"It's just that whatever you've got going on right now," Daisy said, "you know, this whole fascist caveman deal of yours—it's not going to fly with my girl. So, you need to drop it."

Gunnolf raised an eyebrow and glanced at Sylvie, again, for help with the ridiculous female. The thing he had going on was his personality.

Sylvie pointed at the road this time.

He assumed she was indicating that he should keep his eyes there, instead. It was a wise idea. As panicked as he was over Wren's running away, the last thing he needed was to get them into an accident.

"I am afraid I do not understand," Gunnolf answered, flicking on his turn signal.

"Yeah," Daisy responded, "I was afraid of that, too.

Look, I've got three children at home and I'm going to let you in on a secret. Having kids, raising the little buggers, it's like training wild horses."

"Wild horses?" Gunnolf asked, flooring the gas pedal to cross through a gap in the traffic.

"Uh-huh," Daisy replied. "That's what I said. And this Master and Commander crap of yours, this coming on strong and needing everything to work according to your whims and expectations, it doesn't work when you're raising wild horses. Do you have any idea why?"

"Because they are skittish?" Gunnolf frowned, unsure where the conversation was going.

"That's a decent guess but no. It's because they're stubborn as hell," Daisy told him, "and the little monsters are prone to rebellion. You've got to gentle them into the learning process. So, instead of laying down the law with an iron fist, do you know what you have to do?"

Loki interrupted, briefly, to mention they were maybe fifteen minutes, at the most, behind Gunnolf and Sylvie.

"You have to use a shit-ton of patience and love, instead," Daisy continued. "It's called gentling them. You watch the little animals run around in circles, kicking up dirt, and wearing themselves out. All the while, you're desensitizing them to a blanket and a saddle. Only, it's bedtime and homework—not picking their noses in public, too. You do it all because you care. And because you don't want to have your head kicked in by a hoof in retribution for your stupid, inexcusable behavior someday."

"Daisy," Sylvie said, "I think I like you."

"You must be Sylvie," Daisy responded, using Sylvie's name as if it were the foulest of expletives. "Loki mentioned you over lunch today. So, you like me. What about Wren—do you like her, too?"

"Of course," Sylvie answered, sounding a bit puzzled. "Her mother and I were very close."

"Florence was a great gal," Daisy agreed, "and she raised Wren to be one, too. Now, forgive me, honey, but I'm still a little confused about how things work, here. Lay it out for me—does liking her mean you are through stripping for Gunnolf, or do I still need to be worried about your slutty behavior after we save my friend?"

Gunnolf glanced over at Sylvie's horrified face, wondering why on earth Loki had mentioned it. Was he just being stupid, as usual, or had he not thought enough of Sylvie to care? Either way, it was completely insensitive. After this was all over, he was going to have a talk with his brother—one involving fists and claws.

"You have nothing to worry about from either of us," Gunnolf answered, turning his vehicle into the community entrance. The tires squealed a bit in his haste. "Sylvie does not have an interest in me. Even if she did, my heart would still belong to Wren—she is my mate."

"Mate," Daisy repeated. "Is that the biting thing?"

"Yes," he sighed, realizing just how much he had done to Wren without asking permission or even fully explaining, "that is a part of it."

.

CHAPTER THIRTY-SIX

"This may sound rude, but I'm curious," Wren said, shifting nervously from one foot to the other on the carpet. She had rented a steam cleaner for it just last month. Idle chitchat, providing her uninvited guest was into that sort of thing, seemed way better than getting blood everywhere. "You are far too beautiful to have ended up with Bud. How did it happen–is he a shifter, too?"

The girl stared at her for the painful length of several heartbeats before answering, "Bud is disgustingly human, and beauty is no compliment to me. It's a curse. You're the special one that everybody wants—I'm a failed experiment. Zero potential, not even worth a real name—just a gift to some lecherous old man in return for keeping an eye on you."

A living, breathing person gifted to someone else— the idea was horrifying. Based on physical appearance, the young woman 's age might have made her Bud's daughter, but that clearly wasn't her role. Not after being denied fundamental human rights and passed around like a ham sandwich. Wren looked down at the picture she'd dropped, considering the freedoms afforded her growing up on the mountain. She had been incredibly fortunate, more than she had even imagined, that Florence had done what Freya asked of her.

While this poor thing had no one to protect her, the

naiad agreed.

Wren licked her lips and asked, "What's your name?"

"Three," the girl answered.

"Well, Three," Wren spoke slowly, looking into the woman's violet eyes, "those jerks lied to you, but the mirror does not. You are beautiful, and you're certainly not worthless. Being a shifter is a remarkable thing."

"You're lying." Three shook her head, responding to the news with a brittle laugh. "She says it will never be enough."

"Who says it and enough for what?" Wren questioned, her pulse racing as she silently considered her options.

The usually cramped bedroom suddenly seemed downright claustrophobic. She was certain Three had a bullet with her name on it if she couldn't turn the conversation around. Could she disarm a stranger without a projectile ripping through her body, or getting lodged in some vital organ?

"The voice in my head says so," the girl replied. "She said nothing about me would ever be good enough to make someone want to save me."

"Like Florence did for me—is that why you want to hurt me?" Wren couldn't bring herself to say the words kill me, although, she knew that was the case.

"That's not the only reason," Three admitted. Something flickered in her eyes for a moment—hesitation or regret. "Your mother came from water—your father, too. It's everywhere, from the oceans and seas down to the cells in our bodies. Your mind is learning how to connect with it and manipulate it. The group that wants you to access your powers almost certainly has evil things in mind. Bud says they have a silent partner, one who makes them look like the boy scouts."

"Do you know who this partner is? What about my father?" Wren probed, growing hopeful. Her armed visitor wasn't worried solely about herself—she was worried about others.

That had to be a good sign.

Three remained silent, though the look on her face made it pretty darned clear that she knew.

"Look," Wren said, realizing that fate, the Norns, or chance—whatever—was handing her the opportunity to do something better than just buying time, "I know you're not like them. You're a decent person in horrible circumstances, and I'd like to help you. Please, believe me when I tell you I have no desire to be anybody's weapon. This water monster they want to turn me into—that isn't me."

The girl scratched her nose with one hand, deliberating.

"You already know more than I do about what's going on," Wren coaxed.

Her combat training had primarily been for Gunnolf's peace of mind. She loved the man, but she didn't want to resort to violence—that was a Berserker's answer, not a yoga instructor's. Holding her hands out, palms up, in an open gesture—slow, small movements, nothing the girl could misconstrue, she said, "Why not fill in the blanks for me? Help my friends and me, and I can save you in return."

Three wavered, her eyes flickering from Wren to the pistol in her hand. She bit her bottom lip for a moment before answering, "Bud's not going to like it."

"Who cares?" Wren replied with certainty, "Bud isn't here, and I don't think he's next door, either. If he were, you wouldn't be with me in the first place, would you?"

"No," Three admitted. "I dropped him off at the warehouse for work this morning."

Wren nodded, waiting for the girl to continue. Three's life with Bud was a demon in need of exorcising, a story she had yet to tell another living soul. She could see it clearly in those odd violet eyes—this girl had a once upon a time truly worthy of the Brothers Grimm.

"I..." Three licked her lips nervously. "He gives me a little freedom because we both know, if I leave him, I won't get far. They'll find me and punish me. Then, he will."

"How will they find you?" Wren frowned, leaving the punishment part alone for the moment.

"There's a microchip in my back," she said, "close to my spine."

Wren looked up at the textured ceiling for a moment—the expression from better to bad to worse came to mind. She briefly wondered whether they subjected the poor girl to the procedure in human or canine form, but that was irrelevant. Either way, she had not volunteered, and monsters suddenly seemed too kind a word for these assholes.

It's demeaning and invasive, the naiad insisted, something our mate would never allow. No matter what games he plays with us, we are more than a possession or a toy.

"I'll find a way to get that thing out of you," Wren vowed, silently agreeing with her other half. He had his faults, but Gunnolf wasn't the oppressive monster she made him out to be.

"You're nothing like I thought you were," the girl responded, lowering the gun to her side. "I'm sorry. Jealousy and fear got the best of me. I ought to go now— your friends will be arriving, soon."

"I have a better idea. Why don't you stay and let me put away that weapon?" Wren suggested, holding out her hand. "That way, when they get here, all they will find is me having a chat with my new friend in the living room."

"I doubt they will trust me," the girl said.

"All that matters is that I do," Wren responded

"You'd be better off pulling the trigger. I don't deserve your friendship," Three answered tiredly, pointing the gun at the floor. Once the safety was on and the clip removed, she handed them over.

Wren stashed the weapon in her underwear drawer and took the girl's hand, guiding her down the hallway to the living room. She settled Three into her favorite blue recliner before sinking into the worn couch across from her.

She still looked uncomfortable.

"You know," Wren confided, folding her legs in a cross-legged position atop the cushions, "when I was a little girl, the woman who adopted me swore that everybody's story, no matter how happy or sad, should always start with once up a time."

"How come?" the blonde asked idly, running her fingertips, back and forth, over the soft padding and fabric.

Wren looked at Three's violet eyes and sad face—in some ways she still was a child, but, in some, she was smarter than Wren. This girl wanted to escape a miserable past, while she had been trying to hang on to one.

She was such a fool.

Arrogant Viking, dangerous Berserker Wolf, or sexy Plato reading guy who loved his brother and liked to cook for her: It didn't matter what she called Gunnolf Fenric. Regardless of how she chose to define him, she remained his. Not as some helpless doormat, but as his mate, and he belonged to her, too. Everything else—gods, human monsters, babies—they could figure out together.

"Everyone's story should start with once upon a

time," she answered, leaning forward as if sharing some marvelous secret, "because all the best ones do. Now, tell me yours, leaving nothing out. No matter how ugly or hard it is, I'm here with you. I'm listening. After that, do you know what you and I are going to do? We're going to change it—and we'll pick out a better name for you when you're ready. Something that suits a remarkable, violet-eyed girl."

"Why are you so kind?" Three responded.

"Because I don't want to be a weapon," Wren replied, "and, I was lucky enough to have a mother that taught me the value of kindness."

"Alright." Three gave her a wobbly smile in return. "I'll tell you everything I can. I have to warn you, though, some of my memories are patchy."

"Perfectly understandable," Wren answered. "I've blocked things out, too. Oh, and, Three?"

"Yes?" the girl asked.

Wren unfolded her legs, rubbing away pins and needles in the calf that had fallen asleep. "Will you give me the name of this silent partner teaming up with the boy scouts—and the name of my father?"

The girl nodded and said, "Her name is Freya. And I don't know your dad's name, but I know that he came from Atlantis."

CHAPTER THIRTY-SEVEN

"There's a truck next door and two cars in front of her home," Sylvie said for Loki and Daisy's benefit. "We're parking to block the driveway."

"I want you to search the neighbor's trailer, " Gunnolf told her. "See what you can find while I check Wren's place."

He rolled down the window, sniffing at the air. His mate's scent lingered, even over the foulness of the trash bag by her steps, and he swore he could sense her. He prayed— not to Freya, but to Odin—that it wasn't just wishful thinking, that Wren was still inside and safe.

You made me what I am, he said to the god, which is fairly magnificent, so I am grateful. But I cannot kill my mate, and I cannot lose her—please, let me keep her. I will do anything else that you ask me.

We will, his wolf agreed.

"You should wait for me," Loki insisted. "I am almost there."

"I am not wasting time," Gunnolf answered, his gut churning at the thought of losing Wren.

"You don't have a gun in here, do you?" Sylvie asked hopefully, digging through the glove compartment.

"A pistol has never been my weapon of choice," he answered, hanging up her cell phone and tossing it back to her. If he did have one, she would only shoot Loki with it—

not that he could blame her.

"Nothing but axes and fangs, huh?" Sylvie responded, catching the device. "Forever old school. Let's just hope they don't have any firepower, either."

"Odin made me hard to kill, but I still like a challenge," Gunnolf shrugged, pointing at the lot next door. "Go before we draw too much attention—and be careful."

He walked in between the two cars, coming up the driveway. Daisy's barely had any mileage on it. A quick glance in the window revealed sure signs of motherhood, while Wren's Honda was ancient but neat and kid-free in comparison. It was a dinosaur unaware of its extinction—the same as Gunnolf, according to Loki.

A section where one corner of the concrete had cracked matched the split in her small vehicle's back windshield. Both needed attention and the home beyond them didn't seem that much bigger than her car. He doubted it measured more than eleven hundred square feet on the inside—but it was the sacrifice that had kept Wren's Namaste Nest alive.

He paused on the top step as it creaked, his ears picking up two voices inside. Wren's was sweet and calm in conversation, and the other voice, also a female's, sounded relieved. His heart soared—his mate was still there and unharmed.

"Wren!" He knocked, calling out to her. "Loki and Daisy are on their way. I am sorry—for everything. Please, open the door. I do not wish to knock it down."

As he listened to whispered reassurances inside, Gunnolf thought, for a moment, of his mother. How many sacrifices had the woman made, issues and desires on which his father had refused to budge or listen before she strayed from Gunnar's bed and had Halvdan?

When it is important, we will listen and budge, his wolf said.

The importance to us is immaterial, Gunnolf argued. From now on, her happiness is our only concern.

He heard the patter of Wren's feet approaching the door. The knob twisted, and he found himself face to face with her—those beautiful, expressive eyes and full lips— again. He desperately wanted to grab the little beauty and kiss her. Instead, he reminded himself of all the things she needed.

Independence. Autonomy. Space.

"It was unlocked," she said, giving him a funny look. "Never mind, I'm just glad you're here. There's someone I want to introduce you to."

"The girl with the violet eyes. Loki already mentioned her," he frowned, ducking down to step into a small, charming space decorated in whites and sea blues. Why was this one woman so damned hard to understand? She was acting as if nothing had gone wrong between them—was that a good thing or a bad one?

"The girl's name is Three," Wren corrected, gesturing at the figure in the chair, "and she's my friend. Her colorful eyes are not the only thing unique about her, either—there's a microchip stuck in her back that we need to get out of her."

"Three?" Gunnolf said, keeping his doubts over the tracking device to himself. The creature might be lying for sympathy. "Three is a number, not a name."

The girl twisted, turning her body in Gunnolf's direction. She kept her head downcast as her eyes shifted upward in their sockets, making the briefest of eye contact before shooting down to his feet again.

Her posture was that of dog terrified of a beating.

Or a woman with something to hide, his wolf said.

"I was the third one they made—Three is the only name I have," she answered, defensively.

"That's something she and I are going to correct," Wren told Gunnolf, reaching down to wrap the woman's hand inside her own, "as soon as we figure out what else strikes her fancy. In the meantime, Three has been kind enough to share what she knows about my origins with me. My mother did not abandon me—the group that captured her is the same one that created Three."

"It used to be called Project Elemental," Three said. "Now, it's Project Nemesis."

"Three knows something about my father, too," Wren said. "Apparently, he's part of some elite test group. Scientists have been experimenting on them for a while, trying to figure how their abilities work and if there's some way to recreate or transfer them."

"To what end?" Gunnolf asked, crossing his arms over his chest. So far, everything other than the project's new name was old news. "Nemesis means enemy—whose enemy are they trying to create?"

"Odin's, maybe," Wren answered. "At least, Freya is a silent partner so that would make sense."

"Or this creature is preying on you, using your suspicions to construct a believable lie," Gunnolf replied, fighting the urge to growl.

Three not only had the scent of a dog about her but something else that he couldn't quite place. It was bothersome, yet she seemed to have won Wren's trust in the blink of an eye. Whatever game the young shifter was playing, she would find that an Alpha's trust did not come easily—especially not after seeing how freely she courted the touch of that Alpha's mate.

"He doesn't believe us," Three remarked in a soft

voice, maintaining possession of Wren's hand.

"Of course, he does," Wren assured her, glowering at Gunnolf. "It's just that Loki is the charming, easy-going brother—meanwhile, his job is being dark and broody. He takes it very seriously, which is why his always face looks so mean."

"Untrue, mit hjerte, and you know it," he murmured, deciding to fight the violet fire in a young shifter's eyes with intimacy.

Wrapping possessive arms around Wren's waist, he pulled her willing body back against him. His nose pressed against the top of her head, inhaling apple cider shampoo and the spicy sweetness of the naiad beneath it. He rubbed his palms, and his scent, up and down her arms, drawing goose bumps from her skin.

"My face," he rasped, "is not mean when I take my time, licking and stroking you—when my mate lets me worship her beautiful body and cums for me, repeatedly."

The blonde girl looked up at the contented half-smile on Wren's lips and narrowed her eyes before asking, "And what about the other woman, Sylvie—the one your brother mentioned in the restaurant? Where is she, now—did you do the same things to her body, when you were naked with her, too?"

Gunnolf sighed as Wren stiffened against him. Thanks to Daisy, he already knew what was said in the Tea House.

Apparently, Three had heard it, too.

"I did not," Gunnolf answered, not letting go of Wren, "and she is here."

"Where?" Three asked, pulling her hand from Wren's with a look of panic.

"Sylvie went next door to look around while I came

here," he said.

"You should have said something earlier," Three responded. "This is bad. Bud's paranoid—always worrying about people breaking in and taking things—so the place is booby trapped."

CHAPTER THIRTY-EIGHT

"Booby trapped how?" Gunnolf demanded.

"The twisted human way," Three answered, cringing at the sound of an Alpha's temper. "There's a hidden trigger under the carpet in the back bedroom. It releases a flammable gas when it's pressed down. Step off the trigger, and it sparks a big fuse, somewhere. The gas lights up, and boom—the place is suddenly in flames, maybe even blown sky high."

"Why didn't you mention this before now?" Wren asked the girl as Gunnolf ran outside. She turned and saw Loki and Daisy through the open doorway.

Gunnolf spoke to them briefly before rushing through the neighbor's open gate, with his brother in tow. After an incredibly brief argument involving unsubstantiated claims of similar devices causing explosions at gas pumps, they dialed Sylvie's cell phone.

"There was no reason to mention it," Three defended herself, looking up at Wren with pleading eyes. "Your mate is the one who didn't disclose her presence—I only thought to ask about her because of all his sex talk. Males can't be trusted. If the bond you two share matters to him, why keep her around? He should be telling her to stay away, not bringing her here."

Wren rubbed the back of her neck. Three's logic pecked at her insecurities. She was nothing, physically, not compared to Sylvie—the shifter was gorgeous, with muscles and curves in all the right places. What if he was still just obeying the will of the gods, mating with Wren to try and appease them?

Sylvie loved Florence, not Gunnolf, the naiad nagged. *The girl's paranoia is distracting you from the truth.*

Men still lie, Wren responded. Steven did.

Our mate is more than a man, the voice insisted, *he is an Alpha*—and *he is not the one to put us all in danger.*

"Wren, are you okay, girl?" Daisy interrupted, doubling over to catch her breath after bounding through the door. She stood up, throwing a curious glance at the girl in the chair before jerking a thumb back, over her shoulder, in the direction of the driveway. "There's some serious shit about to go down in the house next door."

"I'm okay," Wren confirmed with a nod.

"Good. Let me bring you up to speed," Daisy answered with her *this is not a good thing* face. "Sexy Sylvie stepped on a switch in the back bedroom. The trailer smells funny. She's still standing, but she can't keep her foot down forever. She has forbidden coming in after her, and the beefcake twins are butting heads over who gets to crash the party."

"They're brothers, not twins," Wren said.

"Are you serious? Out of the entire statement, that's what you're choosing to focus on?" Daisy responded.

Her friend was right—Sylvie was in danger, and Gunnolf and Loki were about to throw their muscular butts smack-dab in the middle of it, too. All because of Wren's stupidity in coming back to the mobile home park in the first place. It was her fault, and her responsibility to fix it—but how?

Water beats fire, the naiad said.

"Is Bud's trailer laid out like everyone else's?" Wren asked Three, hoping their plan was going to work.

"I think so," Three nodded.

"So water pipes run underneath, up into the structure, and the ones in the bathroom are pretty close to the back bedroom. There are also pipes in the laundry room and the kitchen, closer to the front," Wren reasoned hurriedly, looking at Daisy. "I can picture them, Daze—gray plastic just like I've got in here. Maybe I can rupture them with the force of the water and use it to negate the gas, or, at least, prevent the spark from happening, so nothing goes boom."

"Honey," Daisy said, starting to catch on but still doubtful, "we're talking about plumbing, not teapots. Not to mention exposure to God knows what kind of gas. Do you think you have enough of a handle on your superhero shit to pull this off?"

"My father's from Atlantis," Wren responded.

"What the hell does that even mean?" Daisy asked her.

"I have no idea, but it sounds good," she answered. Fear of people dying was a strong emotion. She would figure out how to channel it, feel for the pipes, and learn on the fly. "If I can fling rocks and make waves in a lake, then, dammit, I can do this. It has to work. It's going to work. Period"

"Project Nemesis," Three pleaded, rising out of her seat. "They'll know what you're capable of, after this. They'll come for us. Sylvie's a skank, a whore—you don't owe her anything."

"You can't seriously..." Wren said, genuinely horrified at the woman's suggestion she just let someone die.

"Your mate slept with her," Three insisted. "He

probably still wants her—no one's going to blame you for walking away."

"Hey!" Daisy flared her nostrils and stomped one foot on the carpet, snapping at the violet-eyed girl in a tone she normally reserved for her kids. "No shitting all over her girl power mojo, Little Miss Crazy Pants! You're not poisoning Wren's mind with your nasty attitude—you got that, or do I need to repeat myself?"

"No, ma'am." Three sank back into the chair, her eyes wide.

"That's more like it," Daisy nodded. "Now, you keep your skinny blonde ass parked right there—you don't move until I tell you to."

"That was a tad harsh, don't you think?" Wren muttered as Daisy grabbed Wren by the elbow, dragging her out the front door and making a beeline for Gunnolf and Loki.

The two burly brothers were having a heated discussion in Bud's yard about who was going in after Sylvie. Both of them had taken off their shirts, muscles rippling in preparation for a shift into their slightly less flammable werewolf forms.

"Harsh?" Daisy muttered. "Sugar, that was nothing. You should have heard me after I found out Jamal, Jr. got into a fight at school last week. I channeled Pacino from Scarface so well even Big Jamal was afraid of me. I swear, he tried to hide it, but the man cried a little afterward."

Wren looked closely at her formidable friend for a moment. She blew out a deep breath, shaking some of the tension from her arms, and tried channeling a little of Mama Daisy's bossiness.

"Okay," she announced, marching over to the two brothers, "here's what's going to happen. Nobody but me goes in after her. Water is my super power—got it? Gunnolf, I don't want to hear any stupid arguments from you. Loki, hand me the damned phone."

Once she had the phone, Wren quickly explained her plan to Sylvie, with Gunnolf and Loki listening in. The last thing any of them needed was a startled fox moving her foot too soon.

"I do not like this," Gunnolf told her. "I should be the one in danger, not you."

"You'll get over it—and I love you," Wren told him. She stood on tiptoes to grab his shoulders, pulling his dazed face down for a lingering kiss. Hopefully, it wouldn't be their last. If it ended up that way, at least, Odin might let him get on with his life. At this point, the thought of the war god didn't bother her as much—he seemed far more straightforward with his intentions than Freya.

Wren stopped at the steps to Bud's trailer, inhaling slowly. She closed her eyes, extending her arms toward the water beneath the ground, repeating a mantra from yogic meditation to center herself and focus her intentions: Sohum—I am.

I am, the naiad's voice joined in.

Her body tingled with awareness and energy as she let go of everything. The last vestiges of a barrier somewhere within her crumbled. Stretching out, for the first time, with an unfettered mind, she discovered tendrils of magic, hers for the borrowing, rising from the mountain beneath her feet. Something else touched her, too—the newest piece of the strange puzzle of her identity snapping into place.

We are, the voices whispered, insistently.

"Okay, for now, we are," Wren answered, flexing her fingers.

She temporarily opened herself to the collective

strength of their powerful minds. Nausea rolled through her as the connection locked in place, and a tidal wave of angry thoughts came crashing against her own, threatening to drown her. She struggled against them, desperately, searching for something to latch onto and found a unique presence, there, in the midst the storm.

The rush abated, giving way to understanding.

These were minds, extraordinary ones, that the gods locked away—The Kings of Atlantis. Her father, Metis, was among them.

He would show her what to do.

The earth beneath her trembled as she balled her hands into fists. Envisioning the pipes, she flung her hands open and felt the crackle and pop of each pressurized tube, one after the other, exploding. Her eyes snapped open. Her body pulsed and sang, high with unspeakable energy as she opened the door and stepped inside.

CHAPTER THIRTY-NINE

A shiver ran through Gunnolf as he watched Wren cross the threshold into Bud's mobile home. Not once, not even in her anger or the physical intensity of training had the little woman given anyone a glimpse of the sheer magnitude of energy he now felt pulsing through their bond. His skin tingled and itched from the force of it.

The power Freya wanted to control.

"What did I tell you?" Daisy said. She slid in between the brothers, giving both of their arms a good squeeze. "Our girl's got this."

"I don't recall you telling us anything," Loki teased, giving the mother of three a grin that said *I know you were feeling me up.*

Gunnolf stood in the sunlight, not feeling a bit of it as he watched Wren's progress through the open doorway into shadows. Her feet defied gravity, hovering inches above the carpet in the hallway, and her slender hips curved and swayed with blurry motions. She looked liked some primal goddess dancing through a different time stream.

Her wrists twirled, the fingers above them tracing mystic patterns in the air. Layers of water, mist, and ice began to coat the air and walls.

"Holy shit," Daisy said.

"That ought to take care of the gas problem," Loki admitted, amazement apparent in his voice as the ground beneath the trailer rattled and shook. Thin sheets of ice were forming along the outside walls, icicles evolving to dangle from the roofline in conjunction. "Bro, did you know she could...?"

"This is not just her," Gunnolf growled—his wolf was afraid and uncertain what to do about it. "There is something else with her, another presence—I cannot tell whether she is accessing it, or it is accessing her."

Relax, Wren's voice whispered over the pounding in Gunnolf's ears—it was the sound of his heartbeat. I'm okay.

You better be, he countered with concern, watching her pause in her procession toward the figure waiting in the room at the end of the hall. How are you doing all of this? Are you a god, now?

I don't think so, she replied over the sounds of laughter—several masculine voices, echoing in the wake of his question. You spoke to me first, my love. Your fear called me. Let me go, now, so I can save Sylvie.

"Go," Gunnolf spoke the word, unaware he had even done so.

"Go where?" Loki questioned, looking over at him with concern. "What are you talking about—are you feeling alright?"

Gunnolf clenched his jaw. He kept his eyes glued on the petite figure holding out a hand to Sylvie. The two women paused, exchanging words. What were they saying?

Wren had finally admitted that she loved him—even after Three's attempts to make her doubt his fidelity. Surely, the bond between them was too strong for jealousy, now. It seemed more likely that the immediate threat was the source of all this energy Wren wielded, the same place from which the laughter had come. Was it the gods toying with her, somehow?

"I was not talking to myself," he answered thoughtfully, watching his mate lead Sylvie from the belly of the mobile home. "It was Wren—she felt my fear and replied to comfort me."

"Hold on a minute," Daisy said, "are you honestly telling me that you heard her in your mind?"

"That is not so surprising," Loki shrugged. "They say it happens if the bond between mates is potent enough."

"Well, no thank you to that," Daisy immediately responded. "I do not need to know what Big Jamal is thinking all the time. As a matter of fact, I'm pretty sure that would be grounds for divorce. But I do have some questions about this whole slow motion dance routine of hers."

"So do I." Gunnolf kept his voice quiet, glancing back at Three's face in the trailer window as Wren and a very pale Sylvie traveled down Bud's steps. The neighbors were starting to peer out at them, as well. They would need to leave, soon, before the police came.

"Wren thinks Three wants to help us," he added, "but I prefer not to discuss what has happened in front of her. She has yet to earn my trust."

"Yeah, I'm with you on that one," Daisy nodded, looking over her shoulder at the violet-eyed girl, who darted away from the open blinds. "Number Three said some pretty nasty things about you and Sylvie to try and change Wren's mind. Between you and me, I get the feeling that, as long as it isn't Wren, she's not afraid to let people die."

"A cute little thing like that cannot be all bad," Loki grinned, wagging his eyebrows at them as he walked over to take possession of a wobbling Sylvie, "Given the proper sexual incentive, I guarantee she will change her tune."

"Three's had a rough life," Wren warned the younger Fenric. "Tread carefully with her, or you'll find yourself answering to me for it."

"Is that one ever not horny?" Daisy asked Gunnolf dryly, following him over to Wren.

"No." Gunnolf wrapped his arms tightly around his mate, who let out an exhausted sigh and sagged against him. "Although it is not surprising—most shifters are highly sexed."

"But completely monogamous once happily mated," Sylvie added in a weak voice, leaning heavily on Loki.

So there had been an element of jealousy in the conversation between the two women. Gunnolf's chest swelled with pride at the thought his delectable mate felt equally possessive of him. Her reward would have to wait until later. Wren looked exhausted and Sylvie's metabolism, though quick, still battled the effects of exposure to the dangerous gas.

"Ah, yes, monogamy," Loki responded to Sylvie's comment in mock sadness. "I have heard of it. That dreaded day when the shackles of a mating bond are securely in place, and the indiscriminate penis party finally comes to an end."

"FYI, you dipshit," Sylvie responded with disgust on the tail end of a coughing fit, "that's called growing up. Someday, somebody will make you want to do it."

"Gods, I hope not," Loki said.

"Speaking of shackles," Daisy announced, glancing down at her watch for the first time in hours, "I need to rescue the school from my little hellions. Wren, I'll call you after all the inmates at Camp Daisy have been fed tonight for a debriefing."

CHAPTER FORTY

"Wow," Wren said as she eased into a sitting position, ruffling her hands through her dark hair.

"You are welcome," Gunnolf answered, with a devastating smile.

The sheet bearing their combined scents tumbled down her chest and abdomen. She rotated carefully, sliding her legs off the edge of the bed. There was a decided ache in her nether regions and the extra large t-shirt she slipped on rubbed against her overly sensitized nipples.

Insatiable immortal.

"Loki charmed the police force out of investigating," Gunnolf remarked, reaching a lazy hand down to retrieve his boxers. "No one is coming, and you are still tired from wielding all that power, mit hjerte. Stay in bed with me and rest."

"Is that what you're calling it now—rest?" she chuckled, wandering over to the wooden table with its stack of photographs. Possessive as her mate was, she recognized his tactics—he intended to keep her in bed, and away from Three, for as long as she let him. "I'm fine—the only thing wearing me out, now, is some guy doing dirty things to me for the past three hours."

"And he was not finished yet," Gunnolf answered, completely unrepentant. Sweeping across the room in a blur of motion, he slid into a wooden chair behind her, pulling her into his lap.

"He is if he wants me to able to walk," she said, settling against the warmth of his chest. She reached one hand up behind her to caress the corded muscles in his neck.

She had finally owned up to loving him, and it felt fantastic.

"Walking is overrated," he growled, stroking the underside of her arm. "I can carry you everywhere."

"And turn my yoga sessions into tantric sex tutorials? No, thank you," she shivered, her voice coming out more breathlessly than intended.

Her back tingled from where the rumble of his voice resonated through his chest. There was a touch of Alpha in everything he did. She had given him an inch, revealing that she loved him. In return, the beast had exacted several miles of pleasure from her body.

Lucky girl, the naiad whispered.

Her nipples pebbled, goose bumps forming beneath the implication of his fingertips. They were smooth, now, but the claws that had shredded her clothes were still under the surface. From the hints of his wolf she had seen so far, she had no doubt he would be magnificent, fully transformed.

"Are you sure you will not reconsider?" he teased, licking and nipping at side of a delicate neck that belonged to him. "Think of the unparalleled boost in attendance."

She leaned forward, trying not to encourage him, and flipped several pictures over. Her hand paused on the graphic image of a female who was almost identical to her. Though not as unexpected as it might have been before hearing Three's tale, the shock of seeing it still narrowed the world around the photo to a blur.

"My mother," she whispered, turning it over to find a

question mark and the words viable subject. "I don't know her name—my birth certificate was amended when Florence adopted me."

"We will find it together," Gunnolf told her. His voice grew sad as he continued, "I debated hiding her picture but realized I could not. It is better to share a painful truth than to lie to you."

"I've spent too much of my life hiding from things, already," Wren agreed, setting the picture aside to find the second one, which was of equal interest.

We are.

The hulking figures in the tanks housed the minds that had joined with her, offering their unbelievable strength and power, outside the trailer. According to Three, the one time she had seen them in person, they looked just as blurry as they did here. They had been hooked up to screens and equipment, and one of the guards shivered and said *creepy Atlantis fucks.*

She hung on to the photo, twisted sideways in her mate's lap, and demanded, "Tell me, again, what you saw when I was in Bud's trailer. The way I was moving—what did it look like to you?"

He glanced down at the photo and back into her eyes, answering slowly, "It looked like time was moving at a different speed inside the building—you were dancing in slow motion."

"But I didn't slow down anything," she said. "They did. Time felt normal to me, Gunnolf. I was just doing what my father told me—using his equations to manipulate water molecules, nothing else. They were the ones giving me access to something or somewhere—a phase of time where the seconds stretched out enough to give me room to work."

"Making time elastic and turning math into magic—

how is that even possible?" Gunnolf frowned at her.

"I don't know yet, but we're going find out," she responded, giving his nose a triumphant tap with the edge of the picture. "They have all the answers. Just look at them—they're genuinely blurry. It's not a trick of the lens or the light."

"So..." Gunnolf prompted, ignoring the indignity of being swatted on the nose like a delinquent cub.

"So," Wren grinned, squirming on his lap. She was inordinately pleased with herself. "I think it's because of how they were trapped. Legends say the gods supposedly submerged the city in water, removing it from human eyes forever, and it was some stupid punishment for Atlantean arrogance, right?"

"Absolutely," he nodded, pleasantly distracted by the sight of his shirt inching higher over creamy, sex-scented thighs.

"But they're blurry, even away from the city, in containment," she said. "Because they're perpetually out of phase. Water, itself, was nothing new to them. The gods submerged Atlantis—imprisoning them—in Time. They obviously adapted and evolved there, but they're still furious about it."

"I would be, as well," Gunnolf admitted.

"Right," Wren replied. "That part makes sense, but Freya's doesn't. If she wants their power so badly, why not earn their gratitude and loyalty by setting them free? Why would she lower herself to work with human scientists, shoving the kings into jars for use in some convoluted breeding program, instead?"

"Because she is afraid of them," Gunnolf responded, tugging insistently at the edge of the shirt still keeping him from his prize.

"Exactly," Wren answered, "but she isn't afraid of me—I guess she assumes you can control me, even if she can't."

"You are very smart," he replied, "and not naked enough."

"And Freya isn't the only one that's afraid," Wren said, giving in. She stood up next to the chair and lifted her arms, allowing him to pull the offending item from her body. The shirt hit the floor, and the air hit her skin, followed by the warmth of his lips. "I bet all the gods are, which gives us a bargaining chip with Odin. We need to talk to him."

"Mm-hmm. You may be right," he replied, laving a sore nipple with his tongue before seeking out its twin. His fingers fluttered over Wren's belly, moving down toward the cleft between her legs.

"I may be sore—I am right," she responded with a groan as his fingers teased her honey pot.

"You do not feel sore, at all, to me," he remarked with a wicked smile, sliding two of the digits inside of her and pumping them slowly, "and I have given up on the idea of building a pub."

Wren smiled—she was more important than the bar.

"We're so taking a warm, girlie-scented bubble bath together, after this," she grumbled, half-heartedly, melting into him as he picked her up and carried her back to the bed.

CHAPTER FORTY-ONE

"You are exquisite," Gunnolf said, licking his lips. "I swear, I have the tastiest creature in existence in my bed."

"Wolf-tongued flatterer," Wren answered, propping herself up on her elbows and peering out at him from beneath her long lashes.

"Brazen woman," he responded with a wink.

"Uh-uh," she corrected, gesturing, with the crook of a wanton finger, for him to come closer. "I'm the nymph candy that sexed you out of building a bar."

He shut the drawer on the bedside table with a thunk, his hungry gaze never leaving Wren's sexiness. Crawling onto the bed, he stretched out alongside her, with her beloved vibrator in hand, and pressed reverent lips to the soft skin of her abdomen. Her body was steel draped in velvet—she was a firm little yoga-honed goddess with a ridiculous devotion to her silly pajamas.

Their children would sport the same pattern as he tucked them into bed, someday. Of course, they would. It made the perfect argument for having more than one dainty naiad or stubborn wolf. They needed enough to make it worth the cost of hiring a full-time designer to slap goofy cartoons over everything for them. One of the wolves might be even female—they were incredibly rare, but so was Wren—perhaps the first female Berserker, if Odin approved.

"Now that you love me," he murmured lazily

against the warmth of her belly, flipping Mongo's switch. The buzzing toy teased along the inside of one delectable thigh, making her arch and moan. "We need to talk about your discriminatory taste in music."

"Nonsense," she sighed, with an impatient undulation of her hips, "I've always loved you. And, if you're determined that we discuss something right now, that something is going to be Odin."

"No," he rumbled, inching the toy higher against her skin. "It will be Metal."

"Ugh," she responded, biting her lower lip, "Fine—I like Metallica?"

"Viking Metal," he coaxed her. "Like the kind we play in the gym."

"That's noise, not music," she frowned. "Why did Mongo stop moving?"

"You provided the wrong answer," he countered, hiking one eyebrow.

"Half the time, the singers scream," she glared back at him. "No. More than half the time."

"The vocal technique is referred to as growling, not screaming," he reminded her, grazing the moisture that coated her pink outer lips with Mongo's bulbous tip. "Besides, you like my wolf-growl—you think it is sexy."

"Yes," she sighed, "but you're comparing apples and oranges, here. No, not oranges—apples and honey badgers."

"Exquisite as you are, little nymph, he is right," a deep voice suddenly boomed from across the room, "I, myself, have endorsed Viking Metal as music."

Wren sat up, clamping her legs shut as she grabbed a king-size pillow to cover everything she could—something Gunnolf happily noted while swiveling from his seat on the mattress. His fangs and claws dropped, eyes glowing red as he prepared to defend his mate against the bearded god now taking up space at their table.

"You would not win against me," Odin chuckled, pointing at a blushing Wren. "She might, however, in spite of all her pretty pink parts. Needless to say, this makes her of enormous interest to me."

"Of interest, how?" Wren demanded, leaning forward despite a warning palm flattened against her naked shoulder. "Like a lab monkey or a human being?"

"Like the descendant of a bloodline I have forgiven, at Gunnolf's request, in return for help dealing with a few things: Freya, the apocalypse-mongering idiots with which Freya has aligned herself, and, also, the Atlantean Kings," the scarred God answered smartly. He crossed a booted ankle over one knee and leveled the eye he hadn't traded long ago for knowledge in her direction. "My stubborn wife insists I scarred this handsome face to piss her off—I did not. I do, however, know what she has been up to, and, despite it being her idea, I expect the two of you to expand your once upon a time to include children. Providing my son can figure out how."

"I know how to…" Gunnolf blinked, releasing the death grip he had on Mongo as the words my son registered.

The dildo landed, with an indignant whump, on the bed, drawing everyone's attention. Until that moment, the proud Berserker hadn't realized he'd been brandishing his woman's sex toy as a weapon against Odin. It was, without question, the most embarrassing moment of his centuries-long life. Loki could never, ever find out.

"So uptight—you should see your face, right now," the war god laughed, a surprisingly jolly sound from deep within his belly.

It was the same noise that children, born in later

centuries than Gunnolf, attributed to the sly gift-giver, Sinterklaas—a side of the god he had rarely seen. It occurred to him that his late mother, however, had probably seen quite a lot of it, while Odin was busy giving her gifts that a stoic son was better off not envisioning.

"Are you shitting me?" Wren's face mirrored her mate's shock. Otherwise, she gave out mixed signals—hugging the pillow tighter but scooting closer in apparent fascination. "You slept with their mom—does this mean that you're Loki's dad, too?"

"My dear, I have no interest in shitting you," Odin replied, with a wink. "That is my wife's job. And, yes, I slept with their lovely mother—the gods do not believe in divorce, so we establish more flexible rules for ourselves in the bedroom—and Loki is also my son."

"This is huge," she said. "When are you going to tell him?"

"Well," the God answered, his gaze turning serious, "not until I feel he has matured enough to handle it."

"Not anytime soon, then," Gunnolf translated. "Loki attaining maturity will require time and, quite possibly, the most patient woman in existence."

"Essentially," Odin agreed. "He needs to stop sleeping with his therapist, first—the psychobabble, well-intended or not, is annoying. Of course, at the moment, his immaturity works in your favor. I am extending the gift of immortality to your lovely mate, here, in exchange for her silence."

Gunnolf opened his mouth to ask the first in a string of questions. They should talk about how to deal with Freya, what to do about Project Nemesis when those bastards eventually came for Wren, and just what Odin's plans for Wren's father entailed.

"Speaking of daddy issues," Wren preempted him, her eyes aglow with excitement. "With Metis being who he is, does that make me a legitimate Atlantean princess?"

Gunnolf shot the god—his father, as weird as it felt to think it—a pleading look.

"Hard to say," Odin responded, floating to his feet without further ado. "Ask when you hear from him again. It should be soon—the kings are not through with you. Neither am I, but, in this instance, I believe my son's needs—and your naked lessons in music appreciation—take precedence."

Wren's face turned red all over again. This time, the color extended down her neck and into her chest as she asked, "Wait—before you go, what about Three? Can you take care of her microchip?"

"Consider it wiped from existence," Odin said, tapping the side of his nose, "and I'll be in touch. If I were you, I would keep a close eye on that girl—she is not entirely sane and reeks of Freya."

"See? I was right," Gunnolf said as the visiting deity disappeared in a puff of smoke. He kissed his mate's fingers, one by one, and wrestled the pillow away from her. "Relax, mit hjerte. I am confident he is gone—and you need to show me that beautiful body, again."

"You are irredeemable," Wren complained, picking up Mongo. She flipped the switch on her old friend, filling the room with a happy hum before handing the vibrator back to him.

"No. I am not irredeemable," he answered, trailing nips and kisses down her torso with each statement. Odin had been right. He was eager to get started on those children. "I am smitten—enraptured by my beautiful plaything—enthralled by my alluring thrall. From the moment you arrived on my doorstep in those silly pajamas, I knew you were mine."

"And you," she echoed, reaching down to slide off his boxers with a bewitching smile, "you great big Berserker, were meant to complete my once upon a time."

AUTHOR BIO

Jennifer Fales/ J. A. Fales is a Southern California-based author. She possesses a vivid imagination, an adventurous spirit, and a thorough love of yarns, tales, and silly, sexy stories offering hints of otherworldliness and magic. You can find her on Twitter at: https://twitter.com/JenniferFalesCA.

ALSO BY THE AUTHOR

Shadows and Fire
The Seraph Contingency
Sleight of Hand: Shadow Games
The Robusta Incident
Síofra's Tale (short story)
Justice for G (short story)
Let Genesis Come (short story)
The Nymph Before Christmas (excerpt)
The Drifters: Devil May Care
The Van Helstein Gig
Thanx Given: A Peculiar BDSM Fairytale

Dear Reader,

Thank you! You have supported an independent author and, quite possibly, your local bookstore or library by picking up a copy of Chasing Wren's Tale. I sincerely hope that you giggled, blushed, and had as much fun reading the story as I did while writing it. May a little of the magic of Hesiod Mountain cling to your coattails, and may you find a Happily Ever After of your own.

With Much Love,

Jennifer Pales